Thomas Knipe

Report by Mr. Thomas Knipe on the Land Law Act 1881, and the Purchase of Land Act 1885

Thomas Knipe

Report by Mr. Thomas Knipe on the Land Law Act 1881, and the Purchase of Land Act 1885

ISBN/EAN: 9783742812506

Manufactured in Europe, USA, Canada, Australia, Japa

Cover: Foto ©Andreas Hilbeck / pixelio.de

Manufactured and distributed by brebook publishing software (www.brebook.com)

Thomas Knipe

Report by Mr. Thomas Knipe on the Land Law Act 1881, and the

Purchase of Land Act 1885

LAND ACTS (IRELAND.)

REPORT

OF THE

ROYAL COMMISSION

ON THE

LAND LAW (IRELAND) ACT, 1881, AND THE PURCHASE OF LAND (IRELAND) ACT, 1885.

SEPARATE

REPORT BY MR. THOMAS KNIPE.

Presented to both Houses of Parliament by Command of Her Majesty.

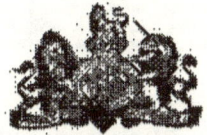

DUBLIN:
PRINTED FOR HER MAJESTY'S STATIONERY OFFICE,
BY
ALEXANDER THOM & CO. (LIMITED),
And to be purchased, either directly or through any Bookseller, from
EYRE and SPOTTISWOODE, East Harding-street, Fetter-lane, E.C., or 32, Abingdon-street,
Westminster, S.W.; or ADAM and CHARLES BLACK, North Bridge, Edinburgh; or
HODGES, FIGGIS, and Co., 104, Grafton-street, Dublin.

1887.

SEPARATE REPORT BY MR. THOMAS KNIPE.

I regret that I have felt compelled to dissent from the report presented by my colleagues for the reasons stated in a letter addressed by me to Lord Cowper with the request that it might accompany their report.

I approve in the main of several of their recommendations, particularly the shortening the judicial term from fifteen to five years, and the immediate revision of judicial rents, the proposal in regard to leaseholders, and other questions to which I refer hereafter. But on the subject of combination among tenants and the recommendations bearing upon the question of social order it appears to me sufficient weight has not been attached to the important evidence which many intelligent and influential witnesses gave us to the causes of agitation and combination.

Mr. Davis, the District Inspector of Castleisland, says—Qu. 21556, 21553—" I believe the purchase of their holdings by the tenants would tend to the preservation of law and order, they would organise to put down outrages themselves; until they do, it will be very difficult and almost impossible to put down outrages—all but impossible because the police are perfectly powerless"; again, Qu. 21547, 21556, 21558—" Unquestionably abatements of rent are necessary. I am informed, and I believe it, that the land did not produce the rent this year. It is not the strength of the League —the people are poorer."

District Inspector Davis

County Inspector Allen Cameron, in charge of County Limerick, says—Qu. 15051, 15054—" I think rents are being paid where any concession is given by the landlord, no matter how small. I think there is no disposition to keep the rents. There is a great deal of boycotting, but I think it is slacking off too. Where no abatement is given the tenants are still inclined to hold out. I think that would be in consequence of the difficulty of making their rents out of the lands; prices are so bad. I think in many instances when they hold out they are not able to pay. I think it is advisable they should have abatements"; and Qu. 15081-15084—" A number of landlords have given reductions on their judicial rents—when this is done the rents are fairly well paid; but where the tenants make application for reduction and it is not granted, they generally hesitate a little and I have known serious outrages to follow that. But altogether the country is in an improved state."

County Inspector Cameron

General Buller, then in charge of the Kerry district, and now Under Secretary for Ireland, says, in reply to Q. 16453, which was—"Do you think that the improved state of the country, so far as payment of rents is concerned, comes from the fact that the power of the League is decreasing ?—No, I do not think so; I think the League would, if they could prevent the payment of rent, and are now endeavouring to their utmost to prevent rents being paid; but the improvement is because the tenants are getting reasonable allowances." And Qu. 16456-16453—"I believe that the great majority of tenants through these counties, that is the majority of those who have not paid, are anxious to pay—when they get reasonable allowances—they must have reasonable allowances."

General Buller

FALL IN PRICES

The report from which I dissent, viewed from my standpoint as a tenant farmer, does not adequately represent the gravity of the situation or the severity of the crisis—a crisis arising not only from the alarming and continuous fall in prices of all commodities on which the farmer has to rely for the maintenance of his family and the payment of rent, but also intensified by the late disastrous seasons and the consequent decreased productiveness of the soil. Now are the effects of the great fall in value of agricultural produce in the failure of a large number of tenants to pay rents fully recognised. From the official returns laid before the Commission by the Registrar General, I find

Reeves, 356 ;
O'Regan, 1594
McElhoy, 9888
Block, 9570 ;
Blackie, 10006 ;
Dickson, 12880 ;
Golding, 13547 ;
Thistleton, 21189
Malley, 27060
McGill ,
Fitzgerald, 36299;
Sheehan, 28925.

A 2

that the estimated value of grain and all other crops in Ireland amounted to in the
years—

	1853,	1881,	and 1886,
	63 millions.	46 millions.	31 millions, sterling.

showing a depreciation in value, in the year 1886, of 32 millions sterling, as compared
with 1873, and 15 millions within the last five years above, or since the Land Act was
passed. The same official returns give the value of the live stock in all Ireland for the
years—

	1881,	1886,
	50 millions.	41 millions sterling.

The following details, extracted from the same valuable statistics of the Registrar
General, show the depreciation in the several items of produce during the same
period :—

Description of Produce.	1881.	1886.	Description of Produce.	1881.	1886.
Wheat, price per 112 lbs.,	10 3	8 1	Hay, price per 112 lbs.,	0 4 4	0 3 3
Oats, „ „ „	8 0	6 8	Straw, „ „ „	0 3 1	0 2 2
Barley, „ „ „	7 6	6 3	Wool, price per lb.,	0 1 11½	0 0 8½
Beans, „ „ „	24 0	35 0	Milch Cows,	15 5 0	14 10 0
Beef, „ „ „	60 3	44 9	Two Year Olds,	12 0 0	9 7 0
Mutton, „ „ „	71 6	46 4	One Year Olds,	7 15 0	4 19 0
Pork, „ „ „	36 0	45 0	Lambs,	0 34 0	0 20 0
Potatoes, „ „ „	4 0	7 3			

It will be seen from the same returns that the combined values of agricultural
produce and live stock for the year 1886, as compared with the average of the four
years, 1881-1884, show a reduction of 23 per cent.
The agricultural rent of Ireland as estimated by Sir John Ball Greene amounts to
about 16 millions sterling. In 1881, therefore, 28 per cent of the total value (say 46
millions) of agricultural produce was due for rent, and in 1886, when the value had
fallen to 31 millions, rent claimed 42 per cent.
If again the value of live stock for 1881 be compared with that of 1886, there will
be found a depreciation of 9 millions sterling in the value of cattle alone, being nearly
three-fourths of the entire agricultural rent payable.

NECESSITY FOR REDUCED RENTS.

When the cost of production is taken into account, it is manifest from the foregoing
figures that the margin remaining for a small struggling farmer after paying all outgoings other than rent, and after his family is supplied with only the barest necessaries
of life, is wholly insufficient to meet rents fixed upon a basis of prices that no longer
exist.
But there is another class of tenant farmers besides that above alluded to who are
unable to pay, and who are patiently but anxiously waiting for relief. Speaking from
my own experience of Ulster, and of the class I represent, I say that farming operations
even upon good land leave no profit, and that for years past rents have been paid
mainly out of the small savings of former years, laid up for a rainy day and for
family emergencies.

Thus, Mr. Ganly, an Antrim farmer, says, Q. 10,250-10,251—" I am not able to pay
rent without going back on the savings of other years. If there does not come some
relief in the way of a reduction of rent or a rise in the price of produce, farmers will
have to give it up. They must go to the wall."

Mr. Golding, a land agent and farmer in Galway, says, Q. 17,347—" The people are
gradually getting poorer, and it is the same with large farmers and small farmers alike.
In fact I could not put my hand upon one either large or small farmer who is not poorer
to-day than he was ten years ago."

Mr. Hobson, who was examined at Cork, says, Q. 19,394-19,405—" I have been
breaking and tilling my farm trying to make the rent out of it. I am not able to pay
my rent out of the place this year. It is paid out of capital altogether. My capital is
gradually dwindling away." And Mr. Osborne, who was examined at Londonderry,

Q. 5026—" Owing to fall in prices, I find great difficulty in paying rent this year. Other
years I have drawn out of savings made before. This year I don't see my way."

Mr. John Browning Heuson, a landlord and agent, farming a good deal of his own Heuson, 15154.
land, says, Q. 15154—" With regard to the judicial rents, I think that in some respects
the last two years were worse years than any we have had before. I think the country
is poorer and more depressed now than it has been yet." And, Q. 15155—" I think they
cannot pay the judicial rents. They really cannot pay any rent at all. They are
exceedingly badly off." And Q. 15158—" I have found the last two years the worst I
ever remember." And Mr. Edward Bennett, Q. 15124—" I know that the land has Bennett, 15124.
been run out of condition in consequence of the poverty of the tenants. They are not
able to till it and to manure it; their capital is gone."

The Land Act of 1881 recognized and legalized the dual ownership in the land that
has always been claimed by the Irish tenants, and it cannot in justice be maintained
that the loss arising from the great and, it is to be feared, permanent decline in prices
should fall entirely upon one of the parties.

The Land Commission returns show that the reductions of rent through the operation
of the Land Courts for the five past years average 18 per cent., but since these rents
were fixed, the official returns of the Registrar-General show a fall in the prices of
produce and cattle equal to 23 per cent. If this were now allowed for, it would give
an abatement of 41 per cent. on the old rents. And it may be observed from the
report of fair rents fixed by the Land Commission in October last, that the 283 cases
decided in that month with an old rental of £7,400 were reduced to £4,400, an abatement of about 40 per cent.

It is scarcely necessary to point out that an additional reduction of twenty-three per
cent. over the former scale does not at all represent the abatement which would fairly
correspond to a fall in prices of twenty-three per cent., since rent is only one of the Maloney, 14181;
many outgoings of a farmer, and to meet this reduced value of the produce a much Thom, 14972.
higher percentage of reduction in his rent would be necessary.

REVISION OF JUDICIAL RENTS.

With respect to the revision of judicial rents, it would, I think, be disastrous if
impoverished tenants were again involved in all the litigation and costs which would Bunt, 15341-
attend fresh applications to the Land Court. The Land Commissioners have by their 15366.
experience gained during the past six years a basis to work upon. They have all the
necessary machinery at hand, and by their Sub-Commissioners could within a limited
space of time inquire into the prices of produce and cattle and the conditions of agri-
culture in each Poor Law Union. Then as reports arrived from each Union the Chief
Commissioners could declare such a reduction per cent. on the judicial rents fixed up
to a specified date as the result of these inquiries by the Sub-Commissioners
warranted.

In the case of non-judicial rents, in order to prevent any sudden influx of applications
and to at once bring home to the poorest class of tenants the benefits which
through poverty or despair they have not availed themselves of, I would suggest that
the Land Commission be empowered to fix a general reduction of rent upon small
holdings, reserving both to landlord and tenant the right to come into Court. Until
some such measures are adopted it is hopeless to expect that combination among
tenants will cease, or that disturbances of an agrarian character can be suppressed,
especially amongst the poverty stricken occupiers of small holdings in the poorer
districts.

A large number of witnesses, comprising landlords and land agents, clergymen,
tenant farmers, and persons in official positions stated before the Commission that a
considerable reduction of rent was necessary.

Mr. Huss, landlord and land agent, said—Q. 15342—" I think it necessary and just Huss, 15342;
to give allowances," and, 15343—" A great many, though offered the allowances, are 15343, 15344.
unable to pay." 15344—" Within the last year or two on judicial rents I have recommended reductions to be given, generally fifteen per cent.; in one or two cases twenty
per cent."

General Buller says, Q. 15451—" My view of the country is this, that the majority Buller, 16451,
of the tenants meant to pay rents, and where they can pay them did pay them, but that 16465, 16471.
the rents have been too high. I do think they are too high." Q. 16453—" I think
they are rents such as they could not pay." And, also, Q. 16471—" I have been lately
in Clare where I have been endeavouring to prevent—Woodford—by suggesting to a

landlord to give reductions. I have not succeeded, and I do not know if I shall; but
in that case I am perfectly sure that some of the judicial rents are too high.'

Mr. Joyce, Agent of Lord Clanricarde, of Woodford, says, Q. 20919—" But I thought
at the time a small abatement might be granted; however Lord Clanricarde did not do
so." Q. 20920—" I was inclined to give them a little abatement." Q. 20922—" I
recommended Lord Clanricarde to give a little reduction." Q. 20923—" And it was in
consequence of that refusal I attribute the very bad feeling that has existed there for
some time past. I think it was wholly so."

COERCIVE LEGISLATION AND COMBINATION.

I think that any attempt to meet agrarian crime and outrage, which unfortunately
prevail in certain districts, by any fresh coercive legislation will now as in the past, not
only fail to secure the tranquility of the country, but will inevitably end in seriously
aggravating the present difficulties.

If the relations which now unhappily exist between landlord and tenant are further
strained, the intentions of the Land Purchase Act will be defeated and sales of land to
tenants, even at lower prices, will be rendered more difficult in many parts of Ireland.
The landlords, with a few honourable exceptions, have failed to meet by prompt reductions of rent the serious fall in prices, or to recognise the serious losses of their tenants,
and to this may be attributed combination and the resistance to evictions which
has taken place, and which might have been averted. If the power of the League is
to be weakened, and the people kept away from combinations which are certain to spread
beyond their present limited area, and thereby endanger further the peace of the country,
it can only be by the Government boldly facing as a whole the Land Question in Ireland,
and by such legislation and government as will convince the poorest of the people that
the Law is their defender and friend.

The Under Secretary when asked before the Commission, Q. 16473—" Would it meet
your idea if when an ejectment was brought into the Court, the Judge of that Court
would have the discretion of saying whether he would evict or not." I replied, " Yes,
that is what I want. It seems to me that it should be his duty to exercise a certain
degree of discretion, but he only exercises it when the tenant comes into Court. Unfortunately, the tenants have been taught that the law is only on one side." Again
Q. 16474-5—" I see some very hard cases. Hard cases of men being pressed for rents
that they could not pay. I wrote to a landlord the other day who was about to turn out
a man, that man paid a year's rent and he owed three—he was evicted, and that man,
I believe, really meant to pay the amount—He was evicted. I satisfied myself that if
he got time he was going to pay his rent, when his children who were in service in
Limerick sent their wages to him." And Q. 16476—" I think that there should be a
discretion in giving decrees, and that there should be some means of modifying and
redressing the grievance of rents being still higher than the people can pay. You
have got a very ignorant poor people, and the law should look after them, instead of
which it has only looked after the rich, that appears to me to be the case coming here."
Also, Q. 16468—" I feel very strongly that in this part of the country you can never
have peace unless you create some legal equivalent or legal equivalent that will supply
the want of freedom of contract that now exists between the landlord and the tenant.
I think there should be some legal machinery which would give the tenant an equivalent for the pressure that the landlord is able to put on him, owing to his love of the
land." Q. 16480-6—" I propose to the Government that there should be a Court, a
permanent Court of Assessors fixed for a certain number of years, who should have
power to raise or lower rents. It would be a Court that would really have a certain
amount of coercive power on a bad tenant, and a very strong coercive power on a bad landlord. It seems to me you want both in this country." And Q. 16487—" There is not
much law in this part of the country, but a short time ago what law there was was really
on the side of the rich."

I venture to say it would be a serious matter with grievances unredressed, to attempt
to suppress by force or fresh coercive legislation the right of tenants openly to associate
for the protection of their interests. A class to whose property the State up to 1891
refused any real legal protection.

LEASEHOLDERS.

f the admission of Leaseholders to the benefit of the Land
air case is a very pressing one. A most industrious class
was fixed in prosperous times. Their exclusion from the

Land Act was unjust and has created in their minds a deep sense of injustice which should be speedily removed.

I recommend that every leaseholder, holding land for agricultural purposes at a rent exceeding the judicial rents fixed on the same estate, or on adjoining holdings, whether for a term of years or in perpetuity, should have the right of going into the Land Court to have a fair rent fixed in the same way as an ordinary tenant from year to year.

Town Parks

I think that the holders of Town Parks should be entitled to apply to the Land Commission to get a fair rent fixed. I cannot see why the population of any town should be taken as a basis from which to exclude the holders of Town Parks from the benefits of the Land Act. Land in some proximity to a thriving and populous town will be more valuable than the Town Parks adjacent to a village. These facts will be taken into consideration by the Commissioners when fixing the rents. The landlord should have power to resume possession of a Town Park under the Commission that the land was bona fide required for building or public purposes, and upon paying to the tenant such compensation for improvements and disturbance as the Court might think just.

Land Purchase

Evidence has been given by many witnesses that tenants have been advised to refrain from purchasing their holdings under the Purchase Acts of 1881 and 1885. In view of the fall in prices, unfavourable seasons, and yearly increasing foreign competition, this advice in my opinion has been justified. It would be a serious matter if tenants were compelled to purchase upon the basis of judicial rents fixed prior to January, 1886, or that they should saddle themselves in all the consequences and improbability of ownership before rents have been re-adjusted so as not only to meet the fall in prices but also to exclude from the rent the value of the tenant's interest and improvement.

I am anxious to see the dual ownership of land in Ireland abolished, and rent converted into a land tax; but purchase upon any large scale can only follow the revision and reduction of rents. It would in my opinion be a serious blunder to exclude the tenants of small holdings from the benefits of ownership.

Labourers' Allotments

Whilst guarding against the subdivision of farms, which is very undesirable, the subletting of a garden or plot of ground by a farmer to any of his labourers residing in or about his farm should not debar him from having a fair rent fixed, as I understand is now done.

Evictions for Nonpayment of Rent

The recommendation of my colleagues that the period for redemption of six months should run from the date of the decree, and not as at present from its execution, would I fear, if carried out, tend to increase agrarian crime in many parts of the country. If such a change were made the landlord would probably in every case allow the term of redemption to expire, and in six months the tenant against whom the decree might have been granted in his absence would find himself out of possession. It would be a most serious change to make in the law in the present condition of the country.

Emigration and Migration.

Although any system of forced emigration, or that would further depopulate the country, would be very injurious, I quite agree with my colleagues that there are many districts where both emigration and migration would be attended with much benefit if brought about by the spontaneous movement of the people. But if the poorer and more backward districts as well as those which are called congested were opened up by tramways and light railways so that the population would naturally circulate before many years, sensible relief would probably be effected, and the wholesale emigration of peoples which has been recommended would be rendered unnecessary.

Mr. Hamilton, Recorder of Cork, who also has been County Court Judge of Sligo and of Carlow, stated before the Commission at Cork, in reply to Q. 18540—"The West of Ireland cannot be improved until it is brought within the reach of civilisation and trade by railroads—by improved communications. It must be done by State aid. I think the natural relief of the place would be emigration, but they will not emigrate." And Q. 18681—"Open up the country; let the people reach the markets; and make their land profitable."

LANDED ESTATES AND LAND COMMISSION COURTS.

I could not assent to any suggestions having for their object the merging of the Land Commission into the Landed Estates Court. There is a deep-rooted prejudice in the minds of the tenant farmers of Ireland, and especially of Ulster, against the Landed Estates Court. They cannot forget the suffering and loss entailed upon them by its action when disposing of encumbered estates, it sold to land speculators the tenants' improvements then unprotected by law.

The Land Commission should be maintained for the settlement of rents, for adjudicating between landlord and tenant, and the transfer of land from owners to occupiers, leaving questions of title and the distribution of the purchase money to be dealt with by the Landed Estates Court.

In conclusion I have great pleasure in saying that I most heartily concur in all that my colleagues have said as to the value of the services rendered by Mr. Hodder to the Commission as its very efficient Secretary.

THOMAS KNIPE.

BELFAST, ARMAGH,
   17th March, 1887.

Thursday, 7th June 1888.

MEMBERS PRESENT:

Mr. T. M. Healy.
Mr. Arthur O'Connor.
Colonel Saunderson.

Mr. Russell.
Mr. Salt.
Mr. Stansfeld.

The RIGHT HONOURABLE JAMES STANSFELD, IN THE CHAIR.

Sir Richard Wyatt.] I HAVE the honour to appear in support of this Bill, which is a measure which has been passed by the other House.

Mr. T. M. Healy.] I respectfully object. I do not know that there is any proposal that the Committee in this case should have counsel attending before them. I think this is a matter for the Committee to decide; and I certainly very strongly object that counsel should be heard here, seeing that there is only one party.

Sir Richard Wyatt.] I am not a counsel, I may mention. I am merely the Parliamentary agent for the Bill.

Mr. T. M. Healy.] Even that, I apprehend, is objectionable.

Chairman.] If you raise the objection I must clear the room.

Mr. T. M. Healy.] Yes, Sir; I do raise it.

The Committee-room was cleared.
After a short time the parties were again called in.

Chairman.] Sir Richard Wyatt, we shall be glad to hear your statement. I do not know whether you intend to call witnesses; probably you do.

Sir Richard Wyatt.] You see, Sir, had this Bill been an unopposed Bill, that is to say, there being no Petition against it, it would have gone in the ordinary course to the Chairman of Committees; and perhaps you are aware that, before that Committee, the usual course is merely to call one witness to prove the recitals and the Preamble; and then, unless the Committee desire further information, it is not usual to trouble them.

This Bill, as I was about to remark, is one that has passed the other House unopposed, and, so far as Petitions are concerned, there is no case here; and, instead of being referred in the ordinary course to the Chairman of Committees, it, as you are aware, has been referred to a hybrid Committee by an Order of the House; and hence the meeting here to-day.

Well, Sir, the object of this Bill is really to consolidate or amalgamate three canal systems; namely, the Lagan Navigation, the Ulster Canal, and the Tyrone Navigation. I do not know whether it would be a convenience to the Committee to know that the Lagan is in length about 27 miles, and the Ulster Canal——

A   Mr.

Mr. T. M. Healy.] Is there a map that we could have, Sir Richard?

Sir Richard Wyatt.] Yes. (*Handing in a map.*) The Ulster Canal is about 44 miles in length, and the Tyrone is five miles; altogether 76 miles. I may mention that the Ulster Canal and the Tyrone Navigation belong to the Public Works Commissioners in Ireland; in other words, it is a Government undertaking; but, unfortunately, that has not been self-supporting. In fact, it entails upon the Government a loss of about 1,000 l. per annum. They have really no funds out of which to provide for the improvement of that navigation with a view to making it pay. They were therefore contemplating the closing of that canal.

Chairman.] Who were contemplating that?

Sir Richard Wyatt.] The Public Works Commissioners, Sir, were contemplating closing the Ulster Canal because it was not self-supporting. The Lagan Navigation is a company. They were very desirous of averting the closing of the Ulster Canal, and they ultimately came to the conclusion that they could by a comparatively small outlay on the Ulster Canal, and working it in conjunction with their own undertaking, make it pay by having the control of the through traffic and by affording facilities to the public, which at present the public have not. Amongst other things, they propose to lower the Ulster Canal, which has a total depth, I believe, of only about four feet of water.

Chairman.] How far do they propose to deepen it?

Sir Richard Wyatt.] To five feet, Sir. They propose to deepen the canal to about five feet, which will admit of the passage of the ordinary craft which pass over the Lagan Navigation.

Mr. Russell.] What depth is it now, Sir Richard?

Sir Richard Wyatt.] About four feet, Sir.

Mr. Arthur O'Connor.] Are you speaking from your own knowledge, Sir Richard?

Sir Richard Wyatt.] I am only making a statement to the Committee, which will be supported by evidence that I propose to call, Sir. It is a statement.

Chairman.] You, Sir Richard, propose to call one witness who will prove the Preamble.

Sir Richard Wyatt.] Yes. I thought, perhaps, it would be a convenience to the Committee to know the position of things. Then, Sir, the Lagan Navigation have put themselves in communication with the Government, and it has ultimately resulted in the Public Works Commissioners consenting, with the sanction of the Treasury, of course, to the transfer of their undertaking, the Ulster Canal, to the Lagan Navigation. Hon. Members are aware that in the House, before the Bill was referred to this Committee, suggestions were made, amongst other things, to prevent the possibility of this canal passing into the hands of a local railway, and thereby depriving the public of the present competition.

Chairman.] Would that apply to all three of the canals, or to the Ulster Canal only?

Sir Richard Wyatt.] I may mention that the Tyrone Navigation is a little one, a very insignificant part of the undertaking; but the Ulster Canal is, as I mentioned, just now, about 44 miles in length. Then, Sir, an arrangement has been come to whereby the transfer is to take place to this Company, and by an Amendment in the Bill we propose to meet the difficulty that was raised in the House of prohibiting a transfer to the Great Northern Railway Company of Ireland. Then there are some lessees who are interested in some of the property of the district, and it was thought it would be an injustice to them if their leases were at all interfered with. That was one of the other points raised by honourable Members in the House.

Chairman.]

Chairman.] Lessees interested in what? In some parts of the Ulster Canal do you mean?

Mr. Russell.] In buildings on the banks?

Sir Richard Wyatt.] Yes.

Chairman.] In buildings on the banks?

Sir Richard Wyatt.] Yes. That point we also propose to meet by amendments in the Bill, a copy of which I believe each honourable Member has. I may mention, Sir, that there appears to have been a consensus of opinion upon this; for meetings have been held in all parts of the locality, and the scheme has, I believe, been unanimously approved of; and it was considered that it would be a great calamity if the Government should abandon this Ulster Canal, and so really cripple the other system in the locality; in fact, it is naturally an integral part of the particular system which, by this arrangement, will be kept open for the benefit of the public.

Then, Sir, the only other point which perhaps I should mention to the Committee, is that the Lagan Canal Company were incorporated for a limited period, and have been from time to time continued by subsequent Acts of Parliament. It is proposed by this Bill now to give them an existence of 999 years, to enable them to keep open this navigation (the Ulster Canal), I may say the consolidated system of the Canal, they hoping that, by judicious management, and having the control of the through traffic, they will be enabled to make it pay, which it does not at present.

Chairman.] Keeping the system open to the sea, I understand?

Sir Richard Wyatt.] No, Sir; not to the sea.

Chairman.] Yes, according to that map.

Sir Richard Wyatt.] No; to the Lough, Sir.

Chairman.] The Belfast Lough?

Sir Richard Wyatt.] Lough Erne.

Colonel Saunderson.] It connects Lough Erne and Belfast?

Sir Richard Wyatt.] Yes; quite so.

Chairman.] What I want to know is this——

Sir Richard Wyatt.] Perhaps Colonel Saunderson will make it plain on the map?

Chairman.] Then the Lagan goes out of the Belfast Lough.

Sir Richard Wyatt.] I have really told the Committee the substance of the Bill and its object. It will be convenient if I now just call a witness, and you can ask him (the witness), and he will explain to you the precise position of things.

Mr. T. M. Healy.] You have not told us on what ground you gentlemen, the Lagan Canal Company, are going to get this free gift of a quarter of a million of money from the State; what are the special terms?

Sir Richard Wyatt.] Perhaps, Sir, you will kindly ask the witness. I can answer the honourable Member by this: that whereas the Ulster Canal has cost a large sum of money it is unproductive, and not only gives no return for the outlay, but entails an annual loss to the Government of 1,000 l. a year, which they are not prepared to continue. Therefore, in pursuance of the power vested in them they would close this, to the great loss and prejudice of the public, and therefore they are willing to give to the Lagan Company the opportunity of seeing whether they could make this undertaking pay.

Mr. Russell.] Sir Richard, may I ask what you propose to do for the lessees in East Tyrone.

Sir *Richard Wyatt*.] You will see an amendment in the Bill, Sir.

Mr. *Russell*.] I beg your pardon.

Sir *Richard Wyatt*.] It is Clause 7, Sir.

Mr. *Russell*.] Yes, I are.

Sir *Richard Wyatt*.] Then I will call the Secretary.

Mr. *Russell*.] Yes; but, Sir Richard, this says that the Company *shall not be prevented* from extending these leases. I apprehend we shall require something stronger than that.

Sir *Richard Wyatt*.] Which Clause are you now on, Sir?

Mr. *Russell*.] I am looking at the end of Clause 7, at the foot-note: "Provided that nothing herein contained shall prevent the Company from leasing or continuing any existing leases subject to the approval of the Commissioners." The case that was made in the House, if I am in order in stating it, was that several of these leases were very near expiring, and that whilst the lessees were quite prepared to trust the Board of Works to have them renewed, they were not quite prepared to trust a private Company who were going to make money out of this business; and I do not think this Clause meets that point at all.

Mr. *T. M. Healy*.] Not at all.

Sir *Richard Wyatt*.] I may mention, Sir, that this has been submitted, as I am instructed, to the lessees, who are content with the Amendment as it stands.

Mr. *Russell*.] All I can say in reply to that is this: these lessees are mainly in my own county of Tyrone; and I most assuredly state here that this does not carry out what I considered to be the arrangement that the Company were willing to come to.

Mr. *T. M. Healy*.] Quite so.

Mr. *Russell*.] It says they shall not be prevented doing it. It does not say they shall do it.

Sir *Richard Wyatt*.] If the honourable Member will be good enough to make any suggestions, so far as the Promoters are concerned, we are quite content to put it in any form as to what you think was intended in the House.

Chairman.] Now we are on the Preamble, will you call your witness to prove the Preamble.

Sir *Richard Wyatt*.] Yes, if you please. When we come to that clause you will perhaps kindly suggest something.

Mr. WILLIAM ROBERT REA, sworn; and Examined.

1. Sir *Richard Wyatt*.] You are, I believe, the secretary to the Lagan Navigation Company, who are promoting this Bill?—Yes.

2. You have read the several recitals in the Preamble, have you?—Yes, I have.

3. Are they true?—Yes, they are.

4. I now, in anticipation of what has fallen from an honourable Member, ask you this. You are prepared, on behalf of the Promoters, to make it quite clear that the interests of the lessees are to be protected, are you not?—Certainly.

Sir *Richard Wyatt*.] Then, Sir, unless the Committee wish to say anything on the Preamble, that is all I propose to trouble you with now.

Mr. *T. M. Healy*.] I should like to ask the Witness a few questions.

5. Mr. *Arthur O'Connor*.] Have you the Lagan Navigation Act of 1843, and the Amending Act of 1873, here?—Yes.

6. Will you let me see them?—Yes. (*The same were handed in.*)

Mr.

7. Mr. *T. M. Healy.*) Are you " William R. Ree," or " William R a "?—
William R. Ree.

8. Is there a Mr. William Ree?—No. It is the same person.

9. Do you remember being examined in 1880 and 1881 before the Royal
Commission?—I do.

10. The members of the Commission, as I understand, were Lord
Monck, Lord Monteagle, Mr. J. Ball Greene, Lieutenant General Burns
Mr. T. A. Dickson, Mr. John Mulholland, Colonel Nolan, and Chief Logan
Tottenham?—Yes, that is correct.

11. Have you read the report of the Commission?—I have.

12. What did they report as to the Ulster Canal?—I think they reported that
it should be abandoned, with the exception of one member (General Dickson),
who protested against that course, and said he thought it ought to get another
trial.

13. Here is the report: " 3.—Ulster Canal.—That it be sold by public competition." Who are your Board?—The Lagan Navigation Company.

14. Have you got a "Thom's Directory" that you can give their names
from?—Do you mean the names of the shareholders?

15. No, the names of the directors?—I can give you their names; they are
John D. Barber.

16. The spinning manufacturer?—Yes; W. A. Robinson, Robert Young, C.E.
and William MacNaughton.

17. How are they appointed?—By the shareholders.

18. At annual meetings, I presume?—Yes, at annual meetings.

19. By what means have they induced the Treasury to assent to this Bill?—
Well, in pursuance of that recommendation, there.

20. The recommendation that it should be sold by public competition?—Yes. The Board of Works advertised it in the different papers, and
invited offers from anyone who would come forward and take it. No one would
come forward to take it, and then they threatened to close it; but, rather than
see it closed, the Lagan Navigation Company came forward, and said they would
make a trial of it, and see if they could do anything for it.

21. Did you offer any money for it?—We did not.

22. Do you know how much it has cost the country?—A little under
300,000 *l.*, I think.

23. And the proposal is, that you should get a gift of this 300,000 *l.* and give
nothing in return?—The proposal is that we should relieve the Government of
the 1,000 *l.* a year, thrown away every year for keeping the canal in its
present useless state, and we guarantee to keep it open and to be at the expense
of keeping it open.

24. But if the Government abandoned the canal, the Government would
lose no more?—But then the country is not willing that the canal system
should be closed up.

25. What do you mean by " the country "?—I mean the traders and those in
the towns along the line of the canal.

26. Are they prepared then to keep it open themselves?—No; they would
much rather the Lagan Company should do it and relieve them of any responsibility, and that they should have the benefit of it without having to pay anything for it.

27. In other words, they want you and the Government to confer a boon upon
them, but to give nothing in return?—Yes, they would certainly be glad to have
it kept open without paying for it if they could manage it.

28. They want other people's money to be spent on their behalf, is that it?—
The Lagan Company is willing to take that risk.

29. When you say the country is not willing that it should be closed, do you
mean that they want to have the money spent for them and to give nothing in
return?—I do not know what they want except that they are very glad to hear
of its being kept open free of expense to them.

30. Are you aware of what has been the net annual income from the canal up
to the present time?—Less than 50 *l.* per annum, or about 50 *l.*

31. *Chairman.*] From the Ulster, do you mean?—Yes.

32. I thought we had it in evidence already that it was a losing concern?—Yes. The expenditure is 1,100 *l.* a-year; the income is about 50 *l.*, therefore the loss is over 1,000 *l.* per annum.

Colonel *Saunderson.*] A loss of 1,100 *l.* a-year.

33. Mr. *T. M. Healy.*] A loss of 1,100 *l.* a-year. (To the *Witness.*) Do you propose to bear that loss of 1,100 *l.* a-year?—No, we propose to try and turn it into a profit by working it in connection with our own navigation.

34. Before I come to that, there is the rental out of the lands?—And the rent is included in that 50 *l.* or 100 *l.* a-year.

35. That cannot be so?—I think it is so.

36. Mr. *Arthur O'Connor.*] Are you speaking from your own knowledge?—Yes, I may say I am.

37. Do you know the amount paid by each of the tenants?—No.

38. Then, you have no knowledge of the fact?—I know the sum total as told me by the Secretary of the Board of Works.

39. Then you are reporting what you have heard?—Yes, but it has been given in evidence.

40. That is only hearsay?—I have heard it given in evidence.

41. Mr. *T. M. Healy.*] According to the report, if I am in order in referring to it, during the five years ending March 1880, the receipts from tolls averaged 50 *l.* (or 55 *l.*), and the rents 131 *l.*; how then can the 50 *l.* include rent and tolls?—The whole thing is not more than about 100 *l.* per annum; the rents and the traffic together.

42. Mr. *Arthur O'Connor.*] How do you know that?—From the Secretary of the Board of Works.

43. Mr. *T. M. Healy.*] Would not the rents be constant?—No, they vary. The rents are all reduced in Ireland now.

44. How is the property held?—How do you mean?

45. How do these gentlemen, who pay rent, hold; is it by lease, or by judicial tenure?—I do not think there are any leases on the Ulster Canal.

46. Perhaps that includes both canals. If that includes both that would account for it.

47. I am to be taken as speaking of both canals?—Probably you would be right as regards both. Perhaps you would be. I was speaking of the Ulster Canal. There is a rent of 50 *l.* alone on Coal Island.

48. Does your company propose then, at any rate so far as the leases go, so far as the rental goes, to take over this rental?—Yes.

49. So that if you took the rental over and did nothing, you would have at least 100 *l.* a year income accruing to the canal?—But then we are bound under the Bill to keep the canal open in a fit state of repair.

50. Supposing you had no money?—We have money. We have ample borrowing powers which we have never exercised under our own Bill.

51. That introduces an inquiry as to your finance. What is your capital?—£. 80,000.

52. Is it nominal or paid up?—Paid up.

53. What are the charges on it?—There is a charge of 300 *l.* a year to the Government; that is all.

54. How are the shares held, are they held in blocks?—In what we call stock, divided in unequal proportions, and held by a number of shareholders.

55. Let me ask you this: all your capital being called up; is it a limited liability company?—No.

56. Then everyone of the shareholders in addition is liable for the debts of the company?—That is a legal point, I suppose, but it is not a limited company.

57. This becomes very important; do you lay it down that to the extent of the debts that may accrue, the shareholders of the Lagan Company will be liable for all the responsibilities according under this Bill?—May I ask you to repeat that?

 st. L

48. Is it your own opinion, or do you lay it down, or do you give the Committee the information as your opinion, that the really bad that will arise out upon your Company of keeping the canal open is that your share-holders will be liable for, so long as he has any property that may be seized?—I don't give an opinion upon that at all; that is an opinion for a lawyer. I only say that our Company is not a limited company.

49. What guarantee has the Committee, supposing they had you on this this property, that is to say, to a company whose shares, as I understand, are full paid up, and as to whose assets or liabilities we practically know nothing, that you will not close the canal next day, on the ground that it was not a paying concern, and had no assets?—We are bound under this Bill not to close. For 20 or 30 years we have paid a small dividend by our own Company, and that has satisfied the Commissioners of Public Works that we are of sufficient standing and position to take over this undertaking.

60. You do not take my point. The Bill is only proper, and there must be some means of enforcing proper besides an Act of Parliament, namely, cash and assets. What I want to get at is the mere fact that you are bound under the Bill; have you any assets by which the obligations under the Bill can be performed and maintained?—Yes; we have our canal undertaking, which is value for 80,000 l., and on which we have always paid a dividend.

61. Do you maintain that if your canal were put up in the market to-morrow it would fetch 80,000 l.?—I do not know what it would bring. There are many things put up in Ireland now that will not bring anything at all.

62. You say that the sole charge on the Lagan Canal, the sole liability you are under now, is 300 l. a year?—Yes.

63. Have you no debts in addition?—Nothing but our annual debts that we square off every year.

64. What are your assets besides the canal: how many lighters have you?—The Company do not own lighters.

65. Are not there lighters on the Ulster Canal and Tyrone Navigation?—The lighters, of course, ply along there, but they are owned by private individuals.

66. Then, except the waterway, you own nothing?—Well, the Company have a steamer on Lough Neagh for towing these lighters.

67. But, beyond the water-way, what are the assets?—The stores and the bed of both.

68. What are they worth?—I do not know.

69. Have you been valued under the Valuation Acts in Ireland?—I suppose we are, for taxes.

70. Would you have any objection to say what poor rate you pay; then we will get at it?—I would not have any objection, if I knew, but I do not know.

71. Have you no idea what the taxes are?—No.

72. Mr. *Arthur O'Connor*.] You are the secretary, are you not?—Yes; but I did not anticipate such a question as that, and therefore did not come prepared to answer it.

73. Mr. *T. M. Healy*.] You ask for power in the 4th Section to borrow on mortgage the sum of 20,000 l. Is that 20,000 l. to be charged on the undertaking which would be granted by the Bill or upon your entire assets?—As I understand, upon the entire undertaking, including the Lagan Navigation.

74. Would you have any objections to insert a provision that the mortgage should not affect the undertaking that you get, but that it should be charged upon your original property?—I think we should be entitled to borrow upon the entire undertaking.

75. You think so?—Yes.

76. Then you think it would be a fair thing that having got a gift of what has cost the State 300,000 l., you should in addition charge it with 20,000 l., which you might lay out upon your original undertaking?—Well, I would not have put it in that way. I would have said, "what is costing the State 1,000 l. a year, and for which they are getting no return."

77. Just allow me to convey my meaning. You will get an asset upon which you can charge 20,000 l., is there anything to prevent you spending that money if you please for the benefit of the original undertaking of the Lagan Company?—I think the purpose for which the 20,000 l. may be used is given in those Sub-sections A., B., C.

78. I am aware of that, but who is to enforce the sub-section?—I do not know.

79. Can you tell me? No, I am not sufficiently versed in Parliamentary matters to know that.

Mr *Richard Wyatt*.] Will the honourable Member forgive me for calling his attention to it. There is an express stimulation as to how it should be applied in the 5th Clause. It is for the purpose of doing so and so and so and so.

80-1. Mr. *T. M. Healy*.] I know; but my point is, If we once hand this over to this body, the Commissioners of Public Works having quite got rid of the charge of this matter, they would not care twopence what becomes of this thing. (To the *Witness*.) Would you have any objection to a clause being put in compelling them to expend this entire sum of 20,000 l. on the undertaking which you get under the Bill?—Yes, certainly; because we may not borrow the 20,000 l. at all. We only take *the power* to borrow; whatever we do borrow we shall be prepared to spend.

82. But to spend it on the undertaking you get under the Bill?—Yes, I do not think we should have any objection to that, subject to these sub-sections. For instance, we are allowed to spend part of it on the purchase of animals and apparatus and other things, and to subscribe to any Company to be worked in connection with the canal. Of course, I mean keeping these provisions in the Bill.

83. I put the question, you know, to the Lagan Company. Will you give a guarantee that any money raised on mortgage shall be spent in the interest of the Ulster Canal and the Tyrone Navigation, and not of the Lagan Company as it at present exists?—We would give a guarantee that any money borrowed under this clause should be spent for the purposes of the clause, and subscribed under the clause.

84. You do not answer my question, you see; will you undertake that your existing Company shall not benefit by the mortgage, but that the mortgage money shall be spent on the Ulster Canal and the Tyrone Navigation works?—That would be doing away with some of the sub-sections here in this Bill.

85. You can answer my question; yes or no?—No, I do not think so.

86. Then, as you would not be willing to do that, why do you provide in the sub-section that the money is to be spent "For giving the Ulster Canal a navigable depth of five feet at least from end to end, and otherwise improving the works thereof; (b) For the purpose of providing, by building or purchase, vessels, animals, and apparatus for the purpose of the carriage and hauling upon the said canals." That includes the existing Lagan Company?—The lighters, that would pass on to the Ulster Canal would first, probably, pass over ours.

87. You have stated you own none?—This gives power to buy them; therefore it would indirectly (I may say directly) contribute to the Lagan Canal.

88. Does the Lagan Canal want "docking"?—No.

89. Lockage?—No, nothing.

90. Is it water-tight?—Yes.

91. Does it want any expenditure of money upon it?—No, nothing, except for the annual wear and tear.

92. Then, apart from the question of animals and apparatus, would you be willing that any money raised on mortgage should not be spent on the Lagan?—Oh, certainly.

93. In 1890, as I understand, the evidence was that the locks on the Lagan Canal and the locks on the Ulster Canal and the Tyrone Navigation were of different widths?—Yes, that is so.

94. And that the lighters on the Lagan were too wide for the Ulster Canal and the Tyrone Navigation?—Yes, that is correct.

95. Does

95. Does that objection or obstruction still operate?—Yes, that is the reason we require to take power to build these lighters, because the present lighters will not go into the Ulster Canal. There are only very few that will and these few we want more.

96. As I understand this scheme now, it is a scheme in effect to knit the two ends of the country covered by the entire water-way?—Yes.

97. And to enable traffic to go up to Belfast?—Yes.

98. How many existing lighters are there?—There are about 70.

99. What is their capital value?—They are valued at about 250 *l.* to 300 *l.* each. They are all owned by private individuals, and I cannot tell their value exactly.

100. Do you propose to build lighters for the purpose of running, what I will call, a thorough water-way?—Yes.

101. How many do you propose to build?—That we have not considered; that would depend.

102. Surely, seeing that the water-way is not wide enough, and that the locks are different, you must have considered what you are going to do?—We would build a certain number and try it, and add more as required.

103. And the trade is at present ribbing 50 *l.* a year?—Trade is impossible upon the canal in its present state.

104. When was trade possible on this canal?—Never in my time.

105. Then can you give the Committee the least idea of what the estimate of your company is of the trade that will accrue to them under this Bill?—Yes, I have prepared the estimate, which is given in that Blue Book. I have not prepared one since, but it is given in the evidence there. It is given in the evidence of R. Adams.

106. What I want to get out is how much money you are going to spend on the lighters?—That is not decided.

107. I think it should be put in the Bill?—We cannot put a thing in the Bill as to which we do not know what will be required.

108. Have you power to build lighters at present?—No, we have not.

109. Then do you take power under the Bill?—Yes.

110. To build the lighters?—Yes.

111. What, roughly, is your estimated traffic?—I could not tell you without the document, but if you will give me a few minutes I will find it for you.

112. That is eight years ago that you are referring to?—Yes; we have never gone into the matter since.

113. Have you not had occasion to consider this?—No.

114. Then are you buying "a pig in a poke?"—No; we are acting upon that; we have the same idea now as we had then.

115. Are any of your Directors here?—Yes; the Chairman is here.

116. Would he be prepared to say what it is estimated at?—No; I think not.

117. Then, do I understand you to say that so little have your Directors considered the only traffic they would propose to get, that none of you can say what is the estimated traffic?—I can give it you from that.

118. That is eight years ago?—It is really an unknown quantity. We cannot be positively certain what traffic we can have. We know that in the towns that run alongside the canals there is a large traffic done, and we know that we can do a fair share of it.

119. Does not the Great Northern Railway run alongside the water-way?—At some parts of it.

120. Then they to some extent, at some places, would be a competing line with you?—Yes, to some points.

121. That would affect your traffic, would it not?—No doubt.

122. Are there any lighters at all at the present time?—Yes, I think there are about eight or nine that will pass into the Ulster Canal now.

123. On the Tyrone Navigation?—On the Lagan.

124. Are they owned by the Government?—No; I own most of them myself.

125. You own them yourself?—Yes.

126. Are there any owned by the Government?—None.

127. Then you would not get any under the Bill?—No.

128. Of course there is nothing to prevent the lighters you own on this navigation passing on into the Ulster Canal?—There is nothing to prevent those specially narrow ones passing into the Ulster. They pass from the one to the other.

129. Your lighters are on the Lagan and not on the Ulster, are they not?—They are on the Lagan Navigation when they are at home, and they pass into the Ulster.

130. They can pass?—About six or eight altogether can pass into the Ulster Canal.

131. Have they ever done so?—Yes.

132. About what point?—As far as Lough Erne. I have had them more than once, and they go to Monaghan pretty often.

133. Then is the canal in a fit state at the present time to enable all this traffic to be done?—No; once in a while you get a chance of going through, but when there is only four feet you have to lighten your boat before you put her into the Ulster Canal.

134. There is a difference of depth?—There is a difference of depth, and also, I may say, at low water there is scarcely any depth at all, and you have to watch your chance to get a boat through. That would not do for carrying on anything like a regular traffic.

135. In those lighters do you carry your own goods?—For the public.

136. What are your charges from end to end?—I can scarcely tell you at the present time.

137. Are they in accordance with the tolls?—Oh, yes. The tolls are very heavy on the Ulster Canal at present. They are three times as much as they are in the Lagan Canal.

138. Three times?—Yes.

139. You, I think, are the gentleman who is principally interested in the passing of this Bill?—I do not know that. The Company is far more interested than I am, I think; I am the secretary.

140. The Company is far more interested, do you think?—I should think they ought to be. I am the secretary of the Company.

141. The Company own no lighters, do they?—No, they do not; but they propose to do so.

142. How many lighters do you own?—I own 14.

143. And can you give any explanation of why it does not pay the Company to own lighters, when it pays you to do so?—They would have owned them long ago, but they had no power under the Acts to own them, and it never occurred in the old days, I suppose.

144. The Company had no power to own lighters in past times?—No.

145. But they had power to allow private individuals to run them?—Yes.

146. Are you prepared to pay anything for getting this gift from the Government?—No; certainly not.

147. Then are you prepared to allow the Government to retain in their own hands any estate or property not connected with the water-way?—I should think we should have no objection whatever to that.

148. Would you then be prepared to agree that the rental, which you say amounts to 100 l. a year, should be paid in relief of taxation in the counties of Monaghan, Fermanagh, and Tyrone?—I do not know about that. That would be a question for the Board. I have not considered that.

149. You only want the water-way, as I take it?—We would require to have the works connected therewith. There is no navigation that ought to be without some surplus land; there is very little here. We require surplus land for putting up stores, or for letting to others who would do that.

150. At any rate, any property not now in your possession. Would you have any objection that the rental for that property, if the Government are going to give you over the water-way, should be paid in relief of taxation in that way?—I think we should. We think the Government is making a very good bargain in getting rid of the loss of 1,000 l. a year, and I think we are entitled to the few pounds a year that come from the property to go towards our loss.

151. Then

151. Then you think you will make a loss of this, do you?—The present loss I spent of? We hope to make a profit, or we would not take it; but it is only a hope. There is the risk of its not making a profit.

152. Do we understand that you would promote a Bill in Parliament at a large expense, and take over this thing if there was much of a risk?—Well I, do not know. I say we hope to make a profit; but there certainly is a risk attached to it.

153. What was the last dividend you paid?—One and a quarter, I think it was. Our average dividend is 1¼ per cent. per annum during the 30 years.

154. Is that on the 80,000 *l.*?—Yes.

155. Does that pay the interest on the money to the Government?—Yes.

156. In your former evidence, at Question 1778, you are asked this: "Assuming that it would be sufficient, and that your estimate of the traffic is correct, so that after paying 1,000 *l.* a year for maintenance there would be a profit of close on 1,000 *l.* a year over and above all expenses, don't you think it would be worth the while of your Company to take the Canal if they could get it for nothing, and to lay out 10,000 *l.* upon it"; and you say, "I think it would"?—Yes.

157. Is that your opinion still?—Certainly. I think it may be worth while to try it, certainly.

158. Then have you no power without the Act of Parliament to raise this money on mortgage?—Not for the purposes of the Ulster Canal. We have ample powers on the Lagan Navigation, which we have not exercised, to raise money, but for the purposes of the Ulster Canal we have no powers, except they are given under this Bill.

159. If your Company consider that, if you get this quarter of a million worth of property for nothing, it would pay you to raise 10,000 *l.* to lay out upon it, then what is to prevent your Company at the present time putting their hands into their pockets and finding 10,000 *l.* without getting any mortgage powers?—The Company, without the present Bill, would not have power to take the Ulster Canal at any price, or expend a penny upon it.

160. I know that, but you are now asking for a mortgage, in addition?—We are asking for power to get money to spend on the Ulster Canal, which we have not got under the present Act.

161. That mortgage would be charged partly on the Ulster Canal, would not it?—On the united system.

162. On the united system?—Yes.

163. Would you be prepared to get power to enable you to raise the 90,000 *l.* on your existing property, without touching the Ulster Canal?—That is a question.

164. You are not prepared?—No.

165. Were you prepared in 1881 to do so?—No.

166. You do not consider that *this* question conveys that answer?—Certainly not.

167. What is the capitalised value of this rental of 120 *l.* or 130 *l.* a year?—I could not tell you at all.

168. You are not prepared to surrender that?—No, certainly.

169. With regard to the leaseholders, have you gone into the question of the leaseholders who hold in Tyrone?—In what respect?

170. Is not the lease of one of the gentlemen nearly run out; the Tile Company?—I have a copy of the rental, if you would like to see it.

171. Will you oblige me with it?—This is it (*handing in the same*).

Mr. T. M. *Healy.*] I think, Mr. Chairman, it would be very desirable that we should have a copy of the rental put in?

Chairman.] Is that it that you have there?

Mr. T. M. *Healy.*] Yes.

172. *Chairman* (to the *Witness*).] You put that in, do you?—Yes, if you wish. (*The document is handed in.*)

0.108.   B 2   173. Then

173. That is the rental of property held by the Commissioners of Public Works?—Yes.

174. Mr. *T. M. Healy*.] If the recommendation of the Royal Commission that this property, instead of being handed to you for nothing, should be put up to public competition, were adopted, can you give any estimate of what it would fetch in the market?—Yes; nothing at all.

175. Would the gentlemen who pay the rental of 150 *l.* give nothing for it? —I am only speaking from what there is public knowledge of, namely, that they invited offers in the newspapers by advertisement, and there was nothing forthcoming.

176. Would the gentlemen, in your opinion, who pay 150 *l.* a year pay nothing to have that 150 *l.* annually extinguished?—I can only speak from what has been done. The Board of Works advertise in the papers asking for offers, and there were no offers coming forward at all. We came forward afterwards and said we would take it.

177. Mr. *Arthur O'Connor*.] For nothing?—For nothing, certainly.

178. Mr. *T. M. Healy*.] In case you failed to work the canal, would you have any objections that the canal should, after a certain period, revert to the local Grand Juries or to any future body that might be appointed to succeed them under a Local Government scheme? It is left in *dubio*, if I may say so. Here is the provision in the Bill at the top of page 4, Clause 3, " (6). The Company shall keep the said canals open for navigation, and in a fit state of repair, and provision may be made for the forfeiture of the said canals by the Company and the reverter thereof to the Commissioners in default being made by the Company in such undertaking." Would you have any objection to say that the " may " should be turned into " shall "?—I do not think so; if we cannot make it a success, we should not care who it goes to after that.

179. Would you have any objections in case you got this canal to undertake that the towns along the banks, or the Grand Juries of the counties, should, as is often provided in the case of Private Bill undertakings with regard to railways where there is a guarantee given, should have some power of appointing gentlemen on the directorate in a modified sense?—I do not think we would agree to that.

180. Would you not allow the Grand Jury of Tyrone, or the Grand Jury of Fermanagh, or the Grand Jury of Monaghan, or the Grand Jury of Derry, to have any representation on your Board?—No. If this canal system is taken over the shareholders of the Lagan Navigation Company, and they alone, would have the right to appoint directors. We would not consent to an outsider coming in to sit on our Board and we have no power to consent.

181. If power was conferred upon you would you be willing to consent?—No; we would not accept it.

182. Then you will take no public supervision of an independent character?—Not of that character, I should think. We are under the supervision of the Commissioners of Public Works.

183. Will you show me how it is to be enforced. Will you point out to me anything in this Bill whereby, if you once get seisin of this Canal, you cannot snap your finger at the Board of Works?—All I can say is that the Board of Works thought that they were sufficiently protected, and that the public interest was sufficiently protected; but I am sure the Company would not object to the supervision of the Board of Works if you wished to put that in in any shape.

184. Who drew the Bill?—The Parliamentary agents, Messrs. Wyatt.

185. Was it submitted to the Board of Works?—It was.

186. Did they make any alterations?—Yes, there were several alterations made in it.

187. You are aware that with regard to the question of the Bann Drainage there is considerable feeling, are you not?—Yes.

188. Would you have any objection to provide that in case the works are made in the Lower Bann, under proposed legislation at the present time, and in case the level of Lough Neagh may be lowered, you shall not be entitled to compensation

compensation?—We have no objection whatever to the level of Lough Neagh being lowered to summer level, which does not injure anybody at all, and that would be quite sufficient for our navigations. We would not ask any compensation for that.

189. The objection is that the locks may be entirely cleared away from the navigation?—The present proposals of the Government are that the water levels shall not be lowered below summer level. There are two distinct propositions regarding it.

190. You said that the proposition of the Government is to lower the summer level?—No; to lower not below the summer level.

191. Then are you acquainted with Bill which Mr. Balfour has yet to introduce?—No, but I know from local information, not received from the Government at all, but from local sources, that the proposition is not to lower below summer level.

192. Then you know that is what the Government intend?—I know that is the idea.

193. May I ask you how you acquired that information?—I have had it from people in the neighbourhood.

194. From common people or from officials?—No, not from officials, not Government officials.

195. Not from Government officials?—No.

196. In case the locks on the Lower Bann are cleared away, and Lough Neagh is reduced below summer level, would you be entitled to compensation?—If that were done the Newry Navigation and the Lagan Navigation would be destroyed, and we would of course require compensation. It would destroy the whole water-way.

197. And would the fact that you had got the Ulster Canal and the Tyrone Navigation into your hands increase your demand for compensation?—I should think it ought to, but it is scarcely worth while making that proposition, because we are quite satisfied with the summer level. The " summer level " does not injure anybody.

198. Would you have any objection to a clause being put in to the Bill to the effect that no works on the Lower Bann or Lough Neagh shall affect or entitle you to compensation?—Not if you add the words, " provided that it be not lowered below summer level," but we should object to its being lowered below summer level, and so would all the other navigations too.

199. Then, practically, if this Bill passes and the Bann is interfered with, you may acquire a vested right to compensation?—No. If this Bill passes the matter is in no worse position than at the present time, because the existing navigations would be ruined, and they would come for very large compensation against the Government.

200. Would you be willing to provide that you should get no increased compensation by reason of the Ulster Canal and the Tyrone Navigation?—I do not think we should.

201. You do not think it would be reasonable?—I do not think it would be reasonable.

202. Then the passage of this Bill might give you a vested interest?—I think that the possibility is so very remote that it is not worth considering.

203. Yet you would not be willing to sacrifice it?—I do not think I should.

204. Colonel *Saunderson.*] I should like to ask you a few questions about the Canal. A report was alluded to, I think, by Mr. Healy adverse to the Canal, was it not?—Yes.

205. Practically speaking, the receipts from the canal have been nil?—Yes.

206. What do you ascribe that fact to?—To the state of the Canal.

207. That is want of water?—Yes. At the best there is only a 4-feet draught, and for a great part of the year there is no reliable passage through it at all. You cannot be sure of getting boats through.

208. And also the leakage of the canal?—Yes, the water runs out through the banks; the banks are leaky.

209. They are not watertight?—No.

210. Was that from the quality of the soil or from want of care in making the canal or keeping it up?—I think there are two points on the canal where it is very much caused by the nature of the soil; the structure.

211. And in that case, to make it watertight, it would require puddling?—Yes, it would.

212. Then in former times did a lighter starting from Belfast or Lough Neagh find difficulty in obtaining access to the towns on Lough Erne owing to shoals?—Yes, very great difficulty. You could not be sure of getting through it.

213. Therefore you could not depend upon the navigation of the Lough for creating assets for the canal?—No.

214. Is that position changed at the present moment?—No, it is not.

215. Is it the case at the present moment that the Government have spent a large sum of money in clearing away shoals in Lough Erne?—Yes; I believe they have spent some 80,000 l., I understand so.

216. Therefore it is the case that shoals, which in former times interfered with lighters proceeding to the towns along Lough Erne, are now removed?—So I understand.

217. Would that, in your estimation, lead to an increase of traffic on the canal?—Yes, I should think it would.

218. Mr. Arthur O'Connor.] Are you speaking from your own knowledge?—Partly from my own knowledge. I have been up at Lough Erne and have had my lighters through there, so that I can speak from knowledge of it.

219. Mr. Russell.] Do you think that if the canal system worked as the Lagan Company is prepared to work, it will be remunerative?—I believe it will.

220. Do you know anything of the opinion of the traders and people in the localities it passes through?—Oh yes. I have records here of meetings held in all the towns interested along the route, and there has been a perfectly unanimous expression of opinion in favour of this Bill passing, and the canal being put in order and not stopped.

Mr. T. M. Healy.] Certainly.

221. Mr. Russell.] Would it be correct to say that these traders and other people in the locality wish this canal system kept open at the expense of the country?—No, they would not wish that.

222. Of course if they send goods, I suppose they want the canal kept open for the purpose of carrying their goods?—Yes.

223. They would have to pay for that, I suppose?—Yes, they would have to pay for that. They would not wish to expend their money on it if they could get anyone else to keep it open without.

224. Is this canal system the only means of regulating the charges of the Great Northern Railway Company?—I do not know whether it is the only means. It is the only competing line.

225. That is what I meant?—Yes, certainly.

226. If this canal system is closed, the Great Northern Railway can change what they like almost throughout the entire province of Ulster, can they not, at least throughout the entire district?—Yes.

Mr. Arthur O'Connor.] "What they like"?

Mr. Russell.] Yes.

Mr. Arthur O'Connor.] Are not there Railway Commissioners?

227. Mr. Russell.] The honourable Member knows that is a very difficult tribunal to get at. (To the Witness.) This navigation is worked now at a loss of 1,000 l. a year to the Government?—Yes.

228. Would you have any objection to insert a clause that if the company proposed at any time to part with this canal it should revert to the Board of Works.

Works, or that notice should be given to public bodies?—No; we should not have any objection to that.

229. You are willing to provide that before the company parts with the canal in any way whatever notice should be given to the public bodies?

Chairman.] With the Ulster Canal?

Mr. *Restell.*] Yes.

Wilson.] No, we have no objection to that.

230. When I say "the public bodies interested in it," I mean such as the grand juries, boards of guardians, and town commissioners, in the various counties through which it runs?—We should have no objection to that.

231. Regarding the lessees of Coal Island, have you any objection to give those people the right to purchase out their interest?—No, I think not.

232. You would be willing to do that?—Yes, we should be willing to do that.

233. And in cases where they declined to do that you would be willing to renew the leases?—Yes; we should be willing to renew the leases, I think, on the present terms.

234. On the present terms?—I think so.

235. You "think" so; are you prepared to do it?—We would be willing to meet them in any matter; at any rate, we should be willing to renew the leases, and not wish to charge them anything on the tenants' improvements, if there is anything in that.

236. I understand a number of the lessees are anxious and willing to purchase their interest. You have no objection to allow them to do that?—No.

237. And, in the other case, can you say that you would be willing to renew the present leases?—We would be willing to renew the leases without charging for tenants' improvements. If the land is of any more value, we might propose to make a little advance upon it.

238. That is hardly the question I ask you. You have got a losing concern in your hand, the representatives of Mr. Robert King or Mr. John Stevenson, for example; Mr. Shsame, the Tile Company, and others at Coal Island have, I have no doubt, greatly improved that property themselves. What I want to know is this: Do you claim the right in renewing those leases to fix a new rent?—Yes, they are satisfied we should do so,

239. On what ground? I am representing them here as well as you, and I want to know on what ground you propose to reserve to yourselves the right to fix a new rent when you have done nothing for the land?—Well, the whole rental is a matter of under 50l. a year.

240. That is a very small matter to the Lagan Navigation Company, but it is a very large matter for the people interested?—I do not believe the Company would quibble about a pound or two a year; that is what it would come to; it would not be more than that.

241. Then are you able to say now on behalf of the Company, that you would renew those leases on the present rents?—Yes, I believe the Company would do that.

242. *Chairman.*] Do we understand you to be authorised to say for the Company that they would?—Yes, Sir, I say that.

243. Mr. *Arthur O'Connor.*] I think you are the Secretary to the Lagan Navigation Company?—Yes.

244. You cannot tell us what the valuation of your own canal is?—I could not tell you off-hand; you mean the Government valuation?

245. Yes?—I cannot tell you off-hand.

246. You cannot tell us what your through rates are, or would be supposing this canal to be open?—I can tell you what our through rates are to ports that are used at present; but I cannot tell you what the rate might be to the Ulster Canal.

247. You have made no estimate?—No, I could not tell you what the rate would be when the canal would be put in order; I can tell you the rates to existing places.

248. You have been connected with the Lagan Company for a good many years, have you not?—Yes, I have.

249. This scheme of taking over the Ulster Canal has been before your mind very often for many years, has it not?—Yes: the Bill has been promoted for four or five years.

250. You made a calculation as to possible traffic, working expenses, and income?—We have made no further calculations since that calculation which is referred to in this Report of the Royal Commission.

251. Have you made calculations with regard to working expenses and the income?—No, we have not.

252. Your Chairman is here, but you say he cannot give any more information than you can?—I did not say so; but I say we have not done that. If you wish to ask the Chairman any question no doubt he will be able to answer it for you.

253. I think you said, in reply to another member of the Committee in regard to certain points upon which you could not give information, that the Chairman was here, but could not give information?—I forget what the question was.

254. Do you remember the answer?—I did say that with regard to one question:—

255. You told us also that the Lagan Navigation Company have no lighters?—Yes.

256. You told us that you, in your individual capacity, own certain lighters?—Yes.

257. And these lighters are employed in working the Lagan Canal?—Yes.

258. And would be employed to work the Ulster Canal?—Yes, some of them; those we could get up there.

259. Under Section 3 of this Bill I see it is proposed that if the sum of 20,000l. or anything under it is borrowed on mortgage by the Company, it may be employed for a variety of purposes, one of which is for the purpose of subscribing to any company or association for carrying goods upon the said canals?—Yes, that is one of them.

260. Is there any reason, therefore, why, if this money, whatever it may be, to borrowed, some of it might not be used by the Company for subscribing to your lighter interest?—I could not tell you what the possibilities are. I do not know at all about that. They could subscribe to any company.

261. That is the proposal, is it not?—I do not know that they ever had any thought of anything of the sort.

262. Certainly not. I am only contemplating remote possibilities; but the fact is that this Bill does provide certain borrowing powers, and that the money raised on those borrowing powers may be, in whole or in part, diverted to subscriptions to external enterprises connected with carrying goods on the canal?—Yes, that is the clause, I think.

263. You, in your private capacity, are the owner of lighters working on the Lagan Canal?—Which would also work upon the Ulster Canal if the Lagan Company obtained it.

264. Did not you say that under your own Bill you have at present ample borrowing powers?—So far as the Lagan Navigation Company is concerned.

265. I believe the Ulster Canal is 44 miles long?—Yes.

266. Have you walked it or traversed it?—I have.

267. You know the land well?—Well, I know the line of the canal well.

268. It varies in width?—Not very much.

269. But still, it does vary?—Yes; but not very much.

270. What is the nature of the land through which it passes; is it good land or bad land?—I think on the 44 miles there is good, bad, and indifferent.

271. Suppose there were no water there and no canal; what do you think would be the area of the land over the whole of that stretch of 44 miles?—I really cannot tell you that; I have not an idea.

272. You have never estimated the superficial area of the land belonging to the canal?—No, I have not.

273. What do you say would be the very lowest estimate of the fee-simple value of the land, as land, apart from the canal undertaking?—I really do not know

know what it would be worth. It would be worth but a trifle, I should say because a narrow strip right through the country would not be very valuable to anybody.

274. How many tens of thousands of acres are there?—"Tens of thousands!" I should not think there would be any "tens of thousands."

275. On that 45 miles?—No, I should not think so. It is a very narrow strip.

276. How many thousands of acres, then?—I say that I cannot give you the area of it at all, but just from my own notion I should not think that.

277. You would not urge that it was less than 1,000 acres, would you?—No, I really could not tell you what it was. I have not made any estimate of it, or measure.

278. It is a very narrow strip. Still the land, as land, good, bad, or indifferent, has a certain value, has it not?—I should think so; some value.

279. And, apart from its workability or unworkability as a canal, in the mere piece of land itself a valuable thing to obtain?—I think the value would be very little unless used as a canal, because, as I say, it is a mere narrow strip running for 44 miles; and I do not know of what use it would be, except for grazing patches.

280. Has it not been already recommended that this canal should be abandoned?—Yes. I think that was practically the recommendation of the Commission.

281. Would it not still remain property of a certain value if it was abandoned as a canal?—Yes; it would still have whatever value there is in the land, I suppose.

282. The Board of Works, I believe, hold it as mortgagees in possession, do not they?—I am not quite certain about how they hold it.

283. You may take it from me that it is so?—Yes.

284. And say that it is a worthless asset, as things stand now?—So they count it.

285. Supposing they came again into the position of mortgagees in possession, on your failing to make it answer, how would their position be benefited?—You see, in addition to the present, they would have the security of the Lagan Navigation. They would have 1,200 l. a year, which would be more than the cost of keeping up the canal, even at the present price, the present annual cost, so that they would be covered.

286. Do you seriously contemplate the possibility of the Board of Works selling or rodlisting the Lagan Navigation Canal in respect of a liability incurred for the working of the Ulster Canal?—Certainly not; because we think we will never give them the opportunity. We intend to try and make it a success.

287. I am asking you to assume that this Ulster Canal proves in the future no more valuable as a working concern than it has proved in the past, and then, on that assumption, do you mean to represent to us that you seriously contemplate the possibility of the Board of Works selling up or foreclosing on the Lagan Navigation Canal?—I do not know at all; I never forecast anything about it. I do not know what they would do. I know that lately they laid hold upon a small railway company in the north that did not come up to its obligations; and perhaps they would do the same thing with us; I suppose they would.

288. Mr. Russell.] As to the value of the land if the canal stopped, it is four feet deep now?—Yes.

289. That would always be a reservoir for water?—It would unless it was filled up.

290. Mr. Arthur O'Connor.] Only half filled up now?—Oh, no.

291. In parts?—Oh, no; it is four feet deep, but there is not always water to fill up the four feet; it would be always there.

292. Mr. Russell.] Suppose the thing was stopped as a canal. I am speaking of the value of the land; it would be always a reservoir for water, would it not?—Certainly, unless filled up.

C

293. And it would cost a great deal more to fill it up than it would be worth, I suppose?—So I should think.

294. Mr. *T. M. Healy.*] May I ask you one or two questions more, please?—Certainly.

295. In your opinion, if the canal were worked, it would hardly affect the drainage of the district?—Not at all.

296. You think there would be no flood? Not at all. I do not think it affects the drainage in the slightest.

297. Have you estimated the cost under your fifth section of giving this depth of five feet, and what that would cost you?—Yes; we have looked into that. It would be something like about 10,000 *l.*

298. Would there not be some stanching to make the canal watertight?—That would include everything.

299. That was the estimate of Mr. King, I think, or of Mr. Adams?—Mr. Adams.

300. Then say 10,000 *l.*; and what rate of interest do you pay; do you borrow the money at four per cent.?—I should think not exceeding four per cent.

301. Four per cent. on 10,000 *l.* is how much?—That would be 400 *l.* a year.

302. And the canal now pays 50 *l.* a year. Do you expect to get traffic to pay the interest on that mortgage of 10,000 *l.*?—Yes, we do expect that.

303. You estimate the traffic at over 400 *l.* a year?—Yes.

304. I see here, with regard to what I said as to the drainage of Lough Neagh, that the following questions were put:—"Question 1505," this is to Mr. Manning: he is the engineer of the Board of Works, is not he?—He is.

305. "Then if you lowered Lough Neagh from two to four feet, you should give up the Ulster Canal Navigation altogether?—(A.) Not necessarily: but if you lowered Lough Neagh, it would involve the construction of another chamber and a lower sill at the entrance of the canal, another at the Lagan Canal, and another at the first lock of the Newry Canal." Then the next question is: "What, in your opinion, would be the probable expense of those locks? (A.) I would not like to give an estimate of that without consideration. (Q.) Roughly, about how much do you think it would be? (A.) I daresay they would cost about 10,000 *l.*" Then, if Lough Neagh were lowered, and you were put to the expense of 10,000 *l.*, would you consider you had any claim upon the Government for that money?—That brings me back to what I said before. If Lough Neagh is not lowered below summer level, all we want to do with the Ulster Canal is included in the 10,000 *l.* If it were lowered below summer level, it would destroy all the navigations existing at present, and the consequence would be heavy claims from all the navigations.

306. How many feet would be necessary to raise this expense, the 10,000 *l.* spoken of by Mr. Manning?—I cannot give you feet or inches.

307. "If you lowered Lough Neagh from two to four feet, you should give up the Ulster Canal Navigation altogether." "No," he says; "but it would involve 10,000 *l.* expense." What is the difference?—But that is not in connection with the Ulster Canal; but that is in connection with all the navigations. The others would require to lower their locks, whether we got the Ulster Canal or not.

308. Would you be satisfied if a provision were put into this Bill, such as is often put into railway Bills, that you would make those repairs, and about increasing the depth, and so on, within a limited time?—In the Ulster Canal, do you mean?

309. Yes?—The intention is to do it within three years, I think.

310. Are you prepared to have that put in the Bill?—I do not that we could object to it; that is to say, unless there should be some obstacle that we did not at all foresee.

311. Five feet within three years?—That is not exactly what I said. I said the intention is to do it within three years, unless some obstacle that we did not at all foresee comes in the way.

312. That being so, I understood you to say you would have no objection to having it put in the Bill?—I do not think we should be bound down to that; we

we cannot get people to carry out contracts in the stipulated time often.   I do not think we should be bound so strictly as that.

313. " Wind and weather permitting."   What is the longest time you would wish?—I think we should have five years if you are going to bind us.   We should not object to five years.

314. Would you have any objection, in case it became desirable under a Local Government system for the town of Belfast, and the surrounding counties of Derry, Monaghan, Fermanagh, and Tyrone, to acquire the entire undertaking as it will now be constituted, to its being provided that it might be so?—Including the Lagan Canal?

315. Yes?—I think we should have to consult our shareholders before giving any opinion upon that point.

316. Have you any guarantee or promise from the Treasury of any sum of money if this Bill passes?—No; we have no guarantee from them at all.

317. When you were trying to pass this as a public Bill, what was the understanding with the Treasury?—In what respect?

318. How many times have you tried to pass this as a public Bill?—Since 1884, it has been in every Session, and never come to a hearing; it was blocked every Session.

319. It was blocked every Session, and very properly?—Except the first time when it passed the Committee after second reading, and came down to the House and was then blocked.

320. Had you any undertaking or guarantee from the Government then that the Treasury would give you any sum of money?—I think not.

321. You think not?—I think not.

322. *Mr. Arthur O'Connor.*] Was there an understanding?—There was an understanding that we should have borrowing powers.

323. *Mr. T. M. Healy.*] Was there any understanding that the Government should make any advance of money?—No, there was not.   There was an understanding that we should have borrowing powers; that was in the Bill.

324. Do you remember Mr. Courtney being Secretary to the Treasury?—I do.

325. Had you any interviews with him?—I think so.

326. Had you any interview with Mr. Jackson, the Secretary of the Treasury?—No.

327. Had your directors?—No.

328. Had you any interviews with Mr. Fowler, Secretary to the Treasury?—Yes.

329. With Lord Frederick Cavendish?—No.

330. Was there no understanding, promise, or undertaking that the Government would lend you money?—Yes, there was an understanding, and there was an undertaking in the first Bill that we should have power to borrow from the Government 10,000 *l.*

331. Were the Government to lend you the money?—They said so.

332. Had you that in writing?—I think so.

333. Would you have any objection to produce the correspondence?—I do not know, I am sure.

334. Have you got it?—I do not think I have it here.

335. *Mr. T. M. Healy.*] Well, Mr. Chairman, as we have power to send for

the Ulster Canal and Tyrone Navigation which you acquire, except with the consent of the Board of Works?—If I understand the question right, if the question is, Would we not take power to change the servants of the Company, the lock-keepers, or others; I certainly say we would not agree to any such thing. We must have power to change any servant we like.

340. That is not my question; my question is, Would you have any objection to joining the Board of Works in all ejectments in respect of the land and tenements you acquire under this Act?—If we take over this canal under this Act, we must have full power of control over the servants of the canal.

341. That is not my question again. Would you have any objection to undertake that the Board of Works should be joined with you in all ejectments you bring in respect of this undertaking?—We do not want the Board of Works or anybody else to join with us after we take over the concern. We must manage it in our own way if we are to make it succeed.

342. Then your answer is that you would object?—Certainly.

343. Would you object to insert a provision in the Bill that in the counties of Tyrone, Monaghan, or any of those adjoining counties through which the canal runs you shall acquire no right of franchise in respect of the proposed Bill?—I did not quite catch the question.

344. You are aware that there is such a thing as a freehold vote, I presume?—Yes.

345. Would you have any objection to providing that the members of the Navigation Company shall acquire no franchise under the Bill?—I do not think we want to interfere as to that.

Sir *Richard Wyatt*.] Perhaps the honorable Member will allow me to remind him that it is impossible that such power should be put in this Bill, this being a private Bill. You cannot alter the general law of the land by a private Bill.

Mr. *T. M. Healy*.] Then my objection remains. Would this Bill confer a franchise.

Witness.] I do not know.

Mr. *T. M. Healy*.] Perhaps you could answer that question, Sir Richard?

Sir *Richard Wyatt*.] Which question?

Mr. *T. M. Healy*.] Would the Bill confer a franchise?

Sir *Richard Wyatt*.] Nothing more than the general law would.

Mr. *T. M. Healy*.] Precisely; does not the acquisition of a taxable freehold in those counties give the right of franchise?

Sir *Richard Wyatt*.] I am unable to say.

346. Mr. *T. M. Healy*.] Quite so. (To the *Witness*.) Would you have any objection to put in the Bill that in case your company becomes wound up, the projects you acquire under this Act should not become an asset in bankruptcy?—I do not catch the meaning of that.

347. Would you have any objection in case your company is wound up or becomes bankrupt, that this asset which you now acquire shall not be put in as a portion of your bankruptcy assets?—I do not know, I am sure.

Sir *Richard Wyatt*.] There, again, Sir, you interfere with the general law.

348. Mr. *T. M. Healy*.] Quite so. (To the *Witness*.) Have you any objection to that?—I do not know really what we could object to.

349. Mr. *Arthur O'Connor*.] I should like to add, with regard to an answer just given, namely, that the navigation traffic would be equal to at least £10 a year, upon what data, speculative or otherwise, is that estimate based? such is based on the estimate that was made some years ago, and on our knowledge of the traffic along the line at the present time, and the traffic to be done at.....

350. When I asked you whether you had made an estimate of the working expenses and the anticipated traffic and the income, you said that you had not made such an estimate?—Yes; I say so still.

351. Now, what do you mean by saying you will have at least 400 *l.* a year?—I say, if the thing is to do any good at all, it must make more than 400 *l.* a year.

352. I do not want you to put it hypothetically:—That is the only way I can put it, because I repeat that we have not made any estimate of it.

353. Then why did you say 400 *l.*, because you said it absolutely without any qualification?—No; excuse me.

354. I will have the question read if necessary; but you unquestionably and without any qualification said you would have 400 *l.* a year, sufficient to cover the interest on the 10,000 *l.*?—I would not say without any qualification that we would have 400 *l.* a year or 400 pence, but I believe that we would have much more than 400 *l.*

355. You did not mention any qualification?—Perhaps you would have the question read.

Mr. Roswell.] He modifies it now, at all events.

356. Mr. Arthur O'Connor.] Now, I will ask you what is the basis of the calculation?—I have told you that.

357. That there is any basis?—There has been no actual estimate made up yet, but from our knowledge of the towns, and of the trade to be obtained from the towns along the line, we think we should make the thing a success and have more than 400 *l.* a year to pay the expenses.

358. I want you to put into words that knowledge which you say justified your estimate?—I do not understand what you want.

359. You have certain knowledge according to which you are satisfied in your own mind that you will have an income of at least 400 *l.* a year; I wish you to convey to us in words what that knowledge consists of?—I cannot convey it to you any more definitely than I have done. I say from our knowledge of the towns and the trade done along the line of the navigation, and from sending lighters occasionally up there, we believe we can make this a success; but nearer than that I cannot go, because we have prepared no estimate of it.

360. It is a sort of floating impression which you cannot reduce into fixed terms?—I cannot come closer than that to it.

361. You can give us no returns showing what the traffic in the neighbourhood is?—No, returns are not possible, because the thing has not been tried.

362. Mr. Salt.] Is there any arrangement or agreement either direct or indirect by which the Company is to receive any money from the Government?—There is an understanding that they are to receive a sum of money from the Government in consequence of relieving them of this 1,000 *l.* a year loss.

Mr. T. M. Healy.] I will take this canal and ask nothing for it. Let that go upon the Notes.

Witness.] We would be very pleased, if you come under the same obligations as the Company, to let you have it.

363. Mr. Arthur O'Connor.] Will you answer the question specifically: How is the 1,100 *l.*, now charged on the Estimates, expended by the Board of Works in connection with the Ulster Canal?—On salaries and maintenance of works.

364. How much for salaries?—I cannot give you the items.

365. How much for maintenance?—I only know from what is made public, the expenditure upon it; but I cannot give you the items at all.

366. Then we are left, as far as you are able to assist us, completely in the dark as to the destination of this 1,100 *l.*?—Certainly; we did not expend it, and have nothing to do with it.

367. Did not you yourself contemplate an expenditure of money in precisely the same way as this 1,100 *l.* has been spent by the Public Works Commissioners?—Yes, but Government money is not always expended so carefully as that of private individuals or private companies.

368. Do you consider you would economise some of that money?—Certainly.

369. How?—I cannot see how the 1,100 l. is spent myself, and judging by the money it costs to keep up our own canal, I have no doubt we could reduce that considerably.

370. How do you think you could reduce that?—I cannot tell you until I see how they are spending it.

371. Would you propose to reduce the expenditure of the 1,100 l. by getting rid of some of the persons who are now receiving annual salaries out of it?—I do not know that. I would require to see who they are; what offices they are fulfilling, and whether they are required or not. We must manage the concern on commercial principles, not to keep pensioners upon it.

372. Mr. Russell.] Do I understand that there is an understanding between the Lagan Navigation Company and the Government that in consideration of the Company taking over this loss they are to get a sum of money from the Government?—Yes.

373. This is the first I have heard of it.

Mr. T. M. Healy.] That is the whole point. I will take it for nothing from the Government.

Colonel Saunderson.] But you would not keep the canal up.

Mr. T. M. Healy.] Certainly not.

Witness.] That is the whole point.

Mr. T. M. Healy.] The whole thing is a swindle from start to finish.

374. Chairman.] Now, Mr. Rea, what is the understanding with the Government?—The understanding is that we should get 3,500 l.

375. You are to get 3,500 l. in consequence of this bargain?—Relieving the Government of the loss of the 1,000 l. a year, but the Lagan Company would be perfectly willing, if any honourable Member wished to have it, and would come under the same obligations, that he should have it. We are only anxious to have it kept open; we do not want it otherwise.

Chairman.] Sir Richard Wyatt, I did not understand you to refer to this in your opening.

Sir Richard Wyatt.] No.

Chairman.] I thought your opening would have covered the whole of the ground, and it now appears that if we had not asked the Witness the question as to this matter, it would not have come to our knowledge.

Sir Richard Wyatt.] Until I have heard it now I was not aware of the fact.

Chairman.] That is a sufficient answer.

Sir Richard Wyatt.] And even now I think there is some misconception, too, on the part of the Witness.

Mr. T. M. Healy.] I think Sir Richard Wyatt should give evidence on oath.

Chairman.] He may by-and-by.

Sir Richard Wyatt.] I believe the honourable Member is an advocate, and he knows that it is not customary to ask counsel or other advocates to be sworn on their statement.

Chairman.] I was not asking any question of Sir Richard Wyatt as a Witness, but rather criticising (as I felt bound to criticise) his opening statement, because it seemed to me that in that opening statement he ought to have adverted to this fact if it was within his knowledge. He now states that it was not within his knowledge, and, so far as he is concerned, I have done with the question.

Sir Richard Wyatt.] That is so, Sir.

376. Chairman.]

376. *Chairman (to the Witness.)* Have you a copy of the Bill?—Yes.

376*. Then please turn to Clause 8, Sub-section (a): "The Company shall undertake to execute, to the satisfaction of the Commissioners, such works of repair, and within such time not exceeding three years from the passing of this Act, upon the said canals, or one of them, as may be specified in the agreement." What is meant by "works of repair"?—It was to put the canal in such a state that it will give a draught of five feet of water for lighters. That is the meaning of Sub-section (a) in Clause 5.

377. *Mr. Arthur O'Connor.*] On the lowest sills; is that the shallowest sills all through? All through.

378. *Chairman.*] Then you have no objection to its being made quite clear in Sub-section (a) of Clause 8 that the "works of repair" include giving the Ulster Canal a navigable depth of five feet at least?—No, that is to say, if it is a practicable thing to do, which we are told it is.

379. I will put it to you in another way; if you turn to Clause 6 you have the power of borrowing 20,000 *l.*, or up to 20,000 *l.*, upon the whole undertaking "for the following purposes or any of them;" there are four purposes, the first is to give the Ulster Canal a navigable depth of five feet at least; if you spend whatever you raise upon the other three purposes you will have nothing for that purpose?—It will be no use to spend money on the other purposes without spending it upon that one, because that is the first.

380. I am right in saying, am I not, that if you spend it upon the others you have no money left for that purpose?—Yes; but there would be no use in the others.

381. Just answer my question?—Yes.

382. Then, as far as the 5th Clause is concerned, you are not absolutely bound to spend any money in increasing the depth of the Ulster Canal?—No.

383. That is so, is it not?—That seems to be so.

384. But I understand you to say that you mean to be bound by Sub-section (a) of Clause 8?—Yes.

385. Therefore, you will have no objection to make that perfectly clear in the wording of that sub-section? No; but it would require the qualification that if there is any impossibility about it, we cannot do it.

386. That is a detail; but you have no objection to that being properly dealt with in that Sub-section (a)?—No.

387. You have been asked what would become of the property if your Company became bankrupt. Turn to Sub-section (b) of Clause 8; if your Company became bankrupt you would no longer be able to keep the canals open for navigation in a fit state of repair?—No.

388. It is proposed to be enacted that "provision may be made for the forfeiture of the said canals by the Company, and the reverter thereof to the Commissioners on default." In so doing?—Yes.

389. I understood you to say, in answer to an honourable Member, that you have no objection to that word "may" being turned into "shall?"—No, I do not think so.

390. That provision "shall be" made in the agreement for the forfeiture of the canals if you do not continue them in a fit state of repair?—No, we have no objection to that.

391. That is what you said?—Yes.

392. Then, I presume, under those circumstances, in the case of such an unfortunate event as the bankruptcy of the Company happening, the canals would revert to the Commissioners?—So it seems.

393. Then, in answer to another question, I understood you to say that the Bill hands over the whole system of canals to the Commissioners in case of your failure to carry out the terms of the agreement under the Bill?—I think it only deals with the two canals, the Ulster Canal and the Tyrone Navigation.

394. I think you said, in answer to an honourable Member (I forget who it was), that you would be bound by the Bill that, in case of failure, the whole

of your undertaking passed to the Commissioners of the Treasury?—I do not remember that.

Mr. *T. M. Healy*.] Yes, it was distinctly stated.

395. *Chairman*.] You did not mean to say so, did you?—No.

396. At any rate, that is not the effect of the Bill as it stands?—No, not as it stands.

397. Mr. *Arthur O'Connor*.] I have asked a question with regard to that, and I understood you to say that the Lagan Company's present property would be chargeable in respect of the amount advanced upon mortgage to the Ulster Canal?—Yes; and in that way it would come to the same thing.

398. Mr. *T. M. Healy*.] But even supposing they made this failure and forfeiture, they would gain by this Bill, under another clause, a renewed lease in respect of the Lagan, although they wholly failed under this Bill; is not that so?—No, I do not understand that.

Chairman.] I want to make clear a former answer. As I read the Bill, in case of failure to keep the system open, they forfeit the canals which they take under this Bill; but they do not forfeit the Lagan Canal.

Mr. *T. M. Healy*.] Quite so; but, on the contrary, as you will see by Section 8, they gain by the continuance of the Lagan Navigation Acts, although they make complete default.

399. *Chairman*.] If your answer to the honorable Member should appear upon the notes to the effect that, in case of failure to keep this whole system open, the whole system, including the Lagan Canal, would be forfeited to to the Commissioners; you did not mean to say so?—No; I did not mean to say so; but it comes to the same thing.

400. Then, with reference to the question of value; if you do not keep the system open, you will have to give it up; and therefore you will retain no portion of the property or of its value?—Yes; I take it to be so.

401. Therefore, you do not receive under this arrangement a property of value, unless you fulfil the conditions of keeping it in a fit state of repair for the use of the public?—Quite so.

402. Mr. *T. M. Healy*.] You stated to my honourable friend here that the canal was extremely narrow?—Yes, it is narrow.

403. Are you acquainted with the Report of Sir John M'Neil, which was made in 1861, in which he says: "The only plan which I can suggest by which any return can be at all obtained from the undertaking is to take off the lock gates and drain the canal, and convert its beds and slopes into grass land, which may be let for grazing. The banks and waste lands, which in many places are of considerable width, may be left for tillage." Are you acquainted with that?—No; but that would not alter it.

404. Are they of "considerable width"?—As far as my knowledge goes they are not; it is a narrow strip.

405. Mr. *Arthur O'Connor*.] You have read *this* report, have you not?—I did read it years ago.

406. You knew that that was in it?—I think I have heard that before; but it does not alter my opinion, and what I said before.

407. Mr. *T. M. Healy*.] As regards the traffic, are you aware what the traffic was before the railways were made?—No, I am not.

408. Are you aware that in 1851 the Ulster Canal was leased to Mr. Dargan the splendid or well-known railway contractor?—Yes, and I heard that Dargan played into the hands of the railway company, and destroyed the traffic by the canal.

409. Mr. *Russell*.] I suppose the trade has largely increased since 1851?—Yes.

Mr. *T. M. Healy*.] Has the population increased? It has not.

410. Colonel

410. *Colonel Saunderson.*] Is it not the case that at that period to which Mr. Healy alludes, the canal was in such a condition that it could not pay, owing to the defective depth of water at the other end of Lough Erne?—I believe so.

Mr. *T. M. Healy.*] With regard to that, I think I should read what has been said upon that point in the Report of the Royal Commissioners: "The Loan Commissioners, as the principal mortgagees, took possession of the property in 1851, and leased it first to the late Mr. Dargan, and subsequently to the Dundalk Steam Navigation Company. On the expiration of the company's lease in 1865, the canal was vested by Act of Parliament in the Commissioners of Public Works. It was then in a very bad condition, and had become almost derelict, and the Board laid out between 1865 and 1873, when it was again open for traffic, 23,000 l. on works of restoration and improvement. The amount of traffic on the canal since 1873 has been insignificant. During the five years ending March 1880 the average annual receipts from tolls were 55 l., and from rents 131 l.; total, 186 l. The average annual expenditure on the canal during the same time was 1,153 l.; average annual deficit, 967 l.; but, as the tolls are, in fact, the only index of the utility of the canal as a means of transit, the rents being paid for lands along the canal belonging to the Commissioners of Public Works, the average annual deficit on the working of the canal has been in reality 1,098 l. If the interest at 3½ per cent. per annum on 147,787 l of public money which has been expended on the canal be taken into account, the annual loss to the State is 6,159 l. Notwithstanding the large sums laid out by the Commissioners of Works on the canal between 1865 and 1873, amounting, as has been stated, to 23,000 l., it is now, chiefly owing to leakage, in a very unsatisfactory state, and, from want of water, navigable only for eight months in the year. The traffic is also restricted even when the canal is fully supplied with water, by its shallowness, and by the smallness of the locks. The boats in use on the Lagan Canal cannot pass along the Ulster Canal when fully laden; the depth of water in the channel of latter being only 4 feet, whilst on the sides of the locks it is only 3 feet 0 inches."

411. Mr. *Arthur O'Connor.*] I believe the rents alone payable by the tenants will about cover the interest payable on the advance proposed by the Government, will they not?—I should think not; not nearly, I should think.

412. £130. a year?—No.

413. What would be the interest on 8,500 l.?——

414. *Chairman.*] Is that to be an advance or a grant?—That is a grant.

Chairman.] That is a grant, the witness says.

Mr. *T. M. Healy.*] It is sensible to give them a grant because it would be foolish to give them a loan.

Mr. *Arthur O'Connor.*] They get 131 l. in rents alone.

Chairman.] We will now clear the room.

Sir *Richard Wyatt.*] I was going to ask one or two questions of Mr. Rea, Sir. I do not know that it very much matters; but there are one or two points the Chairman is anxious should be cleared up about the borrowing.

Mr. *T. M. Healy.*] Perhaps we may get it from the Chairman himself.

Sir *Richard Wyatt.*] I prefer to get it from the Secretary.

Mr. *T. M. Healy.*] We will call the Chairman probably. I think the Committee will feel inclined to do that, will they not.

Chairman.] We may.

Mr. *T. M. Healy.*] I think it is very desirable.

The Witness withdrew.

The Committee-room was cleared.

After a short time, the parties were again called in.

Chairman.] The Committee will meet again to-morrow, at Twelve o'clock, Sir Richard.

[Adjourned till To-morrow, at Twelve o'clock.

MEMBERS PRESENT:

Mr. T. M. Healy.
Mr. Arthur O'Connor.
Colonel Saunderson.

Mr. Round.
Mr. Stansfeld.

THE RIGHT HONOURABLE JAMES STANSFELD, IN THE CHAIR.

Sir *Richard Wyatt.*] THERE is one point, Sir, that I should like to clear up, upon which my mind was a blank yesterday, namely, about the 3,500 *l*, which the witness said was to be contributed by the Government, and perhaps the Committee will allow me to recall Mr. Rea just to ask him a question upon that one point?

Chairman.] Certainly.

Mr. WILLIAM ROBERT REA, sworn; and further Examined.

415. Sir *Richard Wyatt.*] WILL you be good enough to explain exactly what this payment of 3,500 *l* means, and when it originated, beginning with the Bill of 1884, when I believe Mr. Hibbert was the Secretary to the Treasury?—I am not quite sure whether it was 1884; I think it was 1884.

416. Will you explain to the Committee what took place, and the meaning of the payment of 3,500 *l*?—The original intention in the Bill was to give the Company a loan of 10,000 *l*.

417. *Chairman.*] That is to say, your original proposal?—Yes, that was the original proposal made to the Government, and which they agreed to.

418. Mr. *Arthur O'Connor.*] Absolutely, or under conditions?—Under conditions.

419. What conditions?—That the money would be expended upon putting the canal in order.

420. Expended upon the canal exclusively?—Yes.

421. *Chairman.*] In what year was this proposal made and accepted by the Government?—I believe it was in 1883, probably.

422. Sir *Richard Wyatt.*] It was 1883, I see that Mr. Hibbert's name was in the Bill?—But previously to that the proposition was made with regard to the 10,000 *l*, and then Mr. Hibbert altered that.

423. That was a contemplated loan by the Public Works Loan Commissioners to the Company at the usually low rate of interest of about 3 per cent., or something of that kind?—Yes.

424. Mr. *Arthur O'Connor.*] I do not quite understand what you are referring to. Is this the proposal of 1885, or is it the proposal that was made anterior to that date?—It is the proposal that was in force in 1885.

425. When was that proposal that you now speak of first made?—Previously to Mr. Hibbert being in office at the Treasury.

426. Previously to 1885?—Yes. Previously to Mr. Hibbert being in office at the Treasury, the notion was that we should receive loan of 10,000 *l*. When Mr. Hibbert was in office, I think it appeared by some such remarks as were made yesterday, that if the loan was made they would never hear anything

0.103.   B 2   more

more about it, he said: "Instead of giving a loan, we will give a free grant and have done with the matter," and the Company accepted that.

427. *Chairman.*] That the first proposal of a loan of 10,000 l. from the Public Works Loan Commissioners was accepted by the Government, of which Mr. Hibbert was not a member?—Yes.

428. Mr. *Arthur O'Connor.*] The first proposal, whatever it was?—Yes, I am trying to fix the date. Then he proposed that, instead of giving us loan of 10,000 l., he would make this free grant, and so have done with the matter, so that there should be no risk, in order to fall in with the views of those who had objected, and said if this loan was made it would never be repaid.

429. *Chairman.*] Did that sum ever appear in the Estimates?—I am not sure.

430. Sir *Richard Wyatt.*] It never became payable, because the Act never passed. (To the *Witness.*) I do not think you have made it clear to the Committee why Mr. Hibbert consented to a payment of a sum of 3,000 l. I believe it was to recoup you the additional expenses to which you had been put in having to raise your money in the market, instead of getting it at the low rate?—Yes. If we had borrowed from the public instead of from the Government, we would no doubt then have had to pay a higher price for the money; and, I presume, in consequence of that, and in consequence of the remarks that had been made about the loan not being repaid, Mr. Hibbert thought that he met the difficulty by granting us this 3,000 l.

431. *Chairman.*] Are Mr. Hibbert's reasons for the course which he took within your knowledge?—No.

Mr. *Arthur O'Connor.*] Might we have the correspondence between the Company and the Treasury?

432. *Chairman.*] Can you produce the correspondence between the Company and the Treasury?—I do not think I have it here.

433. Mr. *Arthur O'Connor.*] Will you put it in before the next meeting of the Committee?—Yes, if I can lay my hands upon it I will. There is no objection, I think, to it, if you wish to have the correspondence.

434. Surely, you keep it in some order amongst your papers?—Yes; if I have it here, I will give it you.

435. Will you put in, at the earliest opportunity, all the correspondence between the Treasury and the Company with regard to the terms of transfer?—Yes, if the Committee say it is to be done, of course, it must be done, I suppose.

436. You have possibly, in re-considering the evidence you gave yesterday, come across something that you may wish to qualify. Is there any statement you wish to qualify?—I have not read the evidence through.

437. From memory, you do not wish to modify anything?—No.

438. *Chairman.*] With regard to the understanding of the Company, this agreement on the part of the Treasury, as represented by Mr. Hibbert, exists at the present moment?—Oh, yes.

439. And you rely upon that advance of 3,500 l.?—Yes.

Sir *Richard Wyatt.*] There are one or two points upon which I wish to ask a question upon the evidence of yesterday, if the Committee will allow me, which I think are of importance.

Chairman.] Certainly.

440. Sir *Richard Wyatt.*] The Company have .... it their finances, have they not only to consult friends and others in the district, but the Members of Parliament representing the different constituencies immediately affected by the Bill; you have done it yourself, have you not?—Yes, I have.

441. And is it the fact that you have met with no opposition from any quarter whatsoever?—With the exception of one gentleman, every ....
.... unanimous.

unanimous expression of opinion in favour of the Bill, one of the Members for Cavan, Mr. Biggar.

442. Mr. *Arthur O'Connor.*] Was not Mr. Healy Member for Monaghan during part of the time that this question was afloat?—I do not know; I am speaking of the present time.

443. Is it not a matter of common knowledge?—The Members are quite in favour of it now.

444. Is it not a matter of common knowledge that Mr. Healy was Member for Monaghan during part of the time that has elapsed since the first introduction of this Bill?—Yes.

445. Colonel *Saunderson.*] Did Mr. Healy at that time oppose the Bill?—I am not sure that he did; I do not believe he did; I do not think he did.

446. Sir *Richard Wyatt.*] I believe the honourable Member for Cavan is not opposed to the entire measure?—He stated in the House, I believe, that what he wanted was that we should not sell to the public, and that abuse is now given.

447. But at all the meetings that have been held upon the subject there has been a great unanimity of feeling, was there not?—The meetings have been perfectly unanimous.

448. Mr. *Arthur O'Connor.*] Are you aware whether at those meetings the same gentlemen went from place to place, and that their names are introduced into the report which has been circulated in support of this Bill?—I think it is quite likely; they had to bring the matter before the people in the district, and tell them what was going on.

449. Mr. *Russell.*] Were the resolutions at those meetings moved by the same person?—No, I think not.

450. They were moved by local persons, and traders, and others from each place?—Yes; they brought the subject before them, and there was a perfect opportunity for a free expression of opinion.

451. They went as a deputation?—Yes.

452. Mr. *Arthur O'Connor.*] Were the conditions under which the 10,000 l. was first proposed as a loan conditions which had reference only to the canal?—I think so.

453. They did not contemplate any advance of money to the owners of lighters?—I am not quite certain about that, but the original Bill can be produced with that 10,000 l. in it, I think.

454. Was there any proposal that the whole of the grant that Mr. Hibbert suggested of 3,500 l. should also be exclusively expended upon the canal?—I think the idea was that the 3,500 l. should go to make up part of the 10,000 l. which it was estimated would be required to put the canal in order.

455. And that it should not in any part be diverted to the maintenance of the interests of the lighters?—Certainly.

Mr. W. E. ROBINSON, sworn; and Examined.

456. *Chairman.*] You are chairman of the Lagan Canal Company, I believe?—I am.

457. You have heard the evidence of your secretary?—Yes.

458. And do you concur with his evidence?—Yes, I do, perfectly.

459. Is there anything that you would like to say in addition to his evidence, in presenting your case to the Committee?—I do not think there is anything that I wish to say.

460. You think that he has told everything that you wish to say?—Yes, I think so.

461. Have you got the original Bill with you, the Bill which contains the proposal with regard to the loan of 10,000 l.?—I really do not know.

Chairman (to Mr. *Ren*).] Have you the Bill that was originally promoted, and which spoke of the 10,000 *l*?

(*The Bill was handed in.*)

462. *Chairman.*] I see in the second clause of this Bill one of the enactments is to this effect: "The Company shall undertake to execute, under the supervision of some person appointed by the Commissioners, such works of repair and within such time upon the said canal, or one of them, as may be specified in the agreement." These works of repair would include, would they not, the deepening of the Ulster Canal?—Yes.

463. And were intended to include it?—Yes.

464. Then Sub-section B says: "The Commissioners may undertake to pay to the Company from time to time, on account of the cost of the said works of repair, if executed in a manner approved by the Commissioners, such sums out of moneys provided by Parliament as may be specified in the agreement." Is it referred to there as the maximum sum?—The 10,000 *l*?

465. No. In this Bill, according to Sub-section B of Section 2, it is not a question of loan. "The Commissioners may undertake to pay to the Company from time to time, on account of the cost of the said works of repair, if executed in a manner approved by the Commissioners, such sums out of moneys provided by Parliament as may be specified in the agreement"?—That is to say, we do not want the 10,000 *l*. at once, but we want it in instalments as required.

466. I understand from you and from the secretary that the original proposal, accepted by the Government, was a loan of 10,000 *l*., but that was before this Bill was drafted, was it not?—Yes.

467. When this Bill was drafting, then this proposed loan of 10,000 *l*. was changed into a proposed grant of 3,500 *l*.?—It was 3,000 *l*. originally.

468. Was that change in the agreement between your Company and the Board of Works and the Treasury agreed upon, and come to before this Bill was drafted?—Yes.

469. Therefore this Sub-section B. refers to the grant of 3,000 *l*., and not to the loan of 10,000 *l*.?—Exactly.

470. That fixes the date. The date of this Bill is the 17th of May 1884, and now I understand the original idea of the loan of 10,000 *l*. was changed into so understanding that there should be a grant of 3,000 *l*., which was subsequently raised to 3,500 *l*.?—Yes, with the then secretary of the Treasury.

471. And it was agreed upon in the year 1884?—Yes.

472. I think we are wrong. I have only seen the Bill now for the first time, but looking at the wording of Sub-section B., one would suppose that it was a grant, and when I came to Sub-section C., I find, "The company shall undertake to pay to the Commissioners in consideration for the said transfer, and for such payments as aforesaid, on account of the said works of repair, an annuity for such period, and of an amount ascertained in such manner as may be specified in the agreement." Therefore I think we were mistaken, were we not, in supposing that the proposed loan had changed shape and become a proposed grant before this Bill was drafted?—Yes.

473. This Bill evidently contemplates a loan in respect of which the Company were to pay an annuity?—Yes, interest upon the money.

474. Interest and a sinking fund?—Yes.

475. Will you turn to Section 2, Sub-section B.?—"The Commissioners may undertake to pay to the Company, from time to time, on account of the cost of the said works of repair, if executed in a manner approved by the Commissioners, such sums out of moneys provided by Parliament as may be specified in the agreement." Then the Company undertake to pay to the Commissioners interest upon that.

476. Not only interest, but it is interest and repayments in the shape of an annuity?—It is supposed to pay part of the principal along with the interest, I am not sure about that, but I believe that is the case.

477. Can you tell the Committee more exactly than we have yet heard at what date after the date of this Bill that arrangement was altered by Mr. Hibbert?—In the next year, I think. The date of this Bill is 1884. It was in

1885 that Mr. Hibbert expressed a wish not to make any loan by the Government, but to give a grant of 3,000 l. in lieu of that.

478. When did that grant of 3,000 l. become a proposed grant of 3,500 l.?—It was in the present Session. No, the Bill was prepared before this Session.

479. During the course of negotiations prior to this Session?—Yes.

480. Mr. Arthur O'Connor.] Have you had any estimate of the probable expenditure upon the canal for repairs alone?—We have not, but the Board of Works got their engineer to make an estimate, and the amount was 10,000 l.

481. But then, I suppose, as you are undertaking something new, which involves expenditure, as Chairman of the Board it would fall within your province to ascertain what would be the probable expenditure upon each branch of the works?—That is all specified in this estimate made by Mr. Adams.

482. Who is he?—The engineer to the Board of Works.

483. Can you inform the Committee how much is the estimated cost of the necessary repairs of the canal?—£.10,000.

484. Can you tell the Committee how much of that will go to make new lock gates, and how much in deepening the channel?—The Bill specifies all of that.

485. Can you tell us what it is?—Not for each part.

486. You have not that information by you?—No, I do not think we have. The first considerable item was lowering the gates opening into the canal.

487. Deepening the water on the silts?—Yes; and that was a very troublesome thing.

488. I see that the amount is over 10,000 l.?—£.10,500.

489. Ten thousand two hundred and sixty-five pounds, is it not?—So it is.

490. Have you taken any steps to verify this estimate?—We have not; I think we ought to do. We intend to do so.

491. But, before the introduction of this Bill, you had not?—We had not.

492. This is an estimate based upon the resources of the Board of Works?—Yes.

493. This is the same which the Board of Works would be in a position to do the work for?—No, we had to do the work; they would not undertake the responsibility. We had to do the work and they supplied the money.

494. What was the origin of this estimate; was it made for you, or was it made by the Board of Works?—It was made by the Board of Works.

495. It is the Board of Works estimate for works which might have been executed by the Board of Works itself, with all the resources of the Board of Works?—No; the money is to be given to the Company by the Board of Works for the purposes of making the repairs, which their engineer estimates would be required.

496. Are you acquainted with the history of the Ulster Canal?—Yes.

497. Is it within your knowledge that every estimate made by the Board of Works, or any Public Board which preceded the Board of Works, has been largely exceeded in the actual execution of the works?—I never knew it to be different in any case.

498. Chairman.] Are the Committee to understand that the official estimate has never been sufficient?—I am not speaking of the official estimate.

499. Mr. Russell.] Is not that the general tone of all estimates?—Yes.

500. Mr. Arthur O'Connor.] Have not the estimates in regard to the Ulster Canal been exceeded to an extraordinary degree?—They have.

501. Have you any reason to suppose that there is ground for expecting that this estimate will be in any way different from those which were made under the Navigation Commissioners. I think the title is at any time during the last 100 years?—I may say that we have an engineer upon our Board, I mean upon the Lagan Navigation Company's Board.

502. Has he made an estimate?—No, he has not; we did not like to ask him to do it, but he said he had good reason to believe that it could be done for less money.

503. What were the grounds upon which he gave you that opinion; what were

were his reasons?—There is one level in the canal which just lets the water run through like a sieve.

504. Which level is that; what number?—No. 2

505. Will you show me in that estimate anything on account of Level No. 2; I see Level No. 1, and it passes to Level No. 3; where is the estimate for Level No. 2?—It must be in Level No. 3. It is not confined to No. 3; there are other levels.

506. This estimate does not contemplate any expenditure at all upon Level No. 2?—I believe it does not.

507. Your engineer proposes to make some expenditure, at any rate, upon Level No. 2?—Certainly; it is absolutely necessary.

508. Therefore you contemplate expenditure outside of this estimate altogether?—We hope that it may be done within the money provided.

509. I may regard this estimate, then, in some particulars at least, as incomplete?—It is hardly a competent for me to say that, because I am not a professional man.

Chairman.] It is quite clear that it is incomplete.

510. Mr. Arthur O'Connor.] Up to the time that Mr. Hibbert came into office, it was always in contemplation that whatever money was advanced should be repaid, was it not?—Yes, of course, interest upon it.

511. When that proposal was made of transferring the canal to you, and giving you a lump sum in the way of a bonus, what was the consideration passing from you to the Board of Works in return?—Of course there was a good deal of correspondence.

512. I mean what was the substantial consideration which the Lagan Navigation Company was to give in return for the transfer of the canal to them and the sum of 3,000 l., or whatever it was?—There was no consideration at all.

513. And the proposal was rejected by the House of Commons, was it not?—No; it passed first and second readings, and it passed through Committee, and then there was a change of Government, and the Bill lapsed.

514. It did not pass the House of Commons?—No; not the third reading; it passed the first and second reading.

515. Was it opposed on the third reading?—It never got to that stage.

516. It was blocked, I believe, was it not?—Yes, it was blocked.

517. Amongst your other estimates, have you formed one with regard to the extent of the ground along the whole length of this canal of 44 miles from one end to the other?—No.

518. You cannot tell us within 1,000 acres how much the area is?—No, I could not do that.

519. Have you any idea of what would be the fee-simple value of the land?—Not the slightest; we have no interest in that, because we could not tell the land.

520. Has your attention been drawn to this portion of the Report of Sir John McNeill in 1861, namely, "The only plan that I can suggest by which any return can be at all obtained from the undertaking is to take off the lock gates, drain the canal, and convert its beds and slopes into grass land, which may be let for grazing; the banks and waste lands, which in many places are of considerable width, may be let for tillage." Have you had that report under your observation?—I think I have.

521. Have you any idea of the amount which is available for grazing, or of the amount which is available for tillage?—Not the slightest.

522. Have you formed any estimate of the value of the land which is now in the occupation of tenants under the Board of Works?—I think it must be very slight; we have never heard what it is, but I think there are only some small patches.

523. Such as it is, have you ever formed any estimate of the amount of the value of that property?—No, I do not think it entered into our calculation when we decided upon taking over the canal.

524. Is that property inseparable from the canal?—It is.

525. Why is it inseparable from the canal?—The property is the property of the Board of Works, of the Government, and we can do nothing with the land as long as it has water upon it.

526. I am asking you about the land which is now in the occupation of tenants?—We place no value upon the land on the Ulster Canal.

527. My question to you is why the land, which is now in the occupation of tenants, is inseparable from the canal?—I do not know; if it comes into our hands it will be inseparable, certainly.

528. Is there any reason why you should not take the land of the canal without the land at present in the occupation of the tenants?—I do not know that there is much reason, but we do not place much importance upon that.

529. Does not that land in occupation bring you in a rental of between 100 l. and 150 l. a year?—Not so much as that.

530. What is the amount of the rental?—These matters of detail, I would rather you got from the secretary.

531. As Chairman of the Company, would you have any objection to taking over the canal without this land in occupation of the tenants?—I think so; we must get it as it is.

532. You must have the land for which rent is now paid by tenants, together with the canal?—Yes.

533. Is the land which is in the occupation of the tenants in any way necessary for the purpose of working the canal?—I could not answer that question.

534. Are you aware of the Report of the Royal Commission which sat in 1880 and 1881?—I have heard of it, but I have not read it, I think.

535. Are you aware that they say, "We do not think there is a probability of its being profitably utilised within such a reasonable time as would justify any immediate outlay of public money upon it to put it in order"?—If that is true, we are making a bad bargain.

536. Do you remember that they say further in their report, "In our opinion no more public money should be expended upon it"?—The Government has been spending 1,000 l. a year upon it every year since that.

537. Do you remember that they say, "We recommend that the canal, with all the property attached to it, be as soon as possible offered for sale to the public, for we cannot doubt that, if there is really a fair prospect of its becoming a profitable enterprise as a line of water communication, its value as such will be understood and appreciated in the prosperous and wealthy towns of the north, and will be readily purchased and put into proper working order"?—That is just what we are intending to do.

538. But you do not propose to purchase it, do you?—So much the better for us, clearly; that I entirely agree with; in point of fact, the Government could not have done better with the canal, because there was no one to take it. I am not sure that we should be right in taking it.

539. You, as Chairman of the Lagan Company, say, that you are not sure that you would be right in taking it?—I am not sure.

540. When was your last general meeting of shareholders held in regard to this question?—In the month of April, I believe.

541. Would you tell the Committee what were the proposals submitted for the adoption of the shareholders?—The Bill was laid before the meeting, and the shareholders were asked to give their assent or dissent.

542. Did you inform them, as Chairman, that you were doubtful whether they would be making a good or a bad bargain?—No; we might be making a good bargain. I was, myself, running considerable risk with reference to a considerable portion of the stock.

543. But you did not inform your fellow shareholders at that meeting that you were yourself in doubt as to whether it would turn out a good or a bad bargain?—We said that it was possible it might turn out a bad bargain, but we hoped it would not.

544. The liability of your shareholders is unlimited, is it not?—I do not think there is any liability.

545. Is the liability of your shareholders, as shareholders, unlimited?—I think there is no further liability.

546. Is the liability of your shareholders limited at law?—No, it is not a limited company, it is a company got up under an Act of Parliament, and in point of fact what are now shares were once debentures, and the debenture holders had to be content to take shares for.

547. Mr. *Russell.*] What is the financial state of the Lagan Navigation Company at the present moment, is it a solvent company?—It is.

548. Has it debts to any considerable extent other than current debts?—Not to any considerable extent, except to the Board of Works.

549. Mr. *Arthur O'Connor.*] What is the amount of the debt?—I think it is about 300 *l.* or 400 *l.*?

550. That is the rent, I suppose?—No, the sum due; the sum borrowed from them to carry out certain works.

551. Then, besides being lessees of the Board of Works, you are also indebted to them for money borrowed?—We are not lessees.

552. Surely you pay 300 *l.* a year to the Board of Works, do not you?—That is to the Government.

553. That is the Board of Works, is it not?—Well it is.

554. Mr. *Russell.*] You have no debts other than current debts?—We have a few debentures, about 150 *l.* in the shape of debentures.

555. That is not what I mean; have you any law costs hanging over you?—Nothing, except the law costs, which we will have to pay here under this Bill; we are in a solvent condition. Our receipts are over 4,000 *l.* a year.

556. And you are able and willing to work this canal?—Yes, we are able and willing to work the canal.

557. *Chairman.*] I understand from your evidence that the estimate upon which you have been examined is only for a portion of the necessary works on the whole system?—No, it is an estimate that we got from the Board of Works to see what could be done by way of making it navigable.

558. Does that estimate refer to the Ulster Canal only?—It refers to the Ulster Canal only.

559. It does not refer to your canal?—It has nothing to say to our canal.

560. Do you contemplate any expenditure upon your own canal?—No.

561. Does that estimate include all the works which you propose to undertake under this agreement?—It does.

562. But you are disposed to think that the estimate will be exceeded?—It might be; but I hope not.

563. Did you not say in answer to one honourable Member that this estimate included nothing for the outlay upon Level, No. 2?—No repairs are necessary, because the Board of Works instructed their engineer to go over the whole canal and estimate what would put it into proper repair.

564. Then that is not a level that will need deepening?—No.

565. Then when you take power to raise the sum of money up to 20,000 *l.*, in your opinion, you take a more than sufficient power?—Yes.

566. And supposing that sum to have been raised, you would have no doubt at all about being able to carry out this agreement; is that so?—We will be very careful in borrowing.

567. But my question is this: supposing you had in hand that sum of 20,000 *l.*, which is the limit of your borrowing powers in this Bill, then I understand from you that you feel quite certain of being able to carry these works through?—Yes.

568. Have you any doubt about being able to raise the money upon fair terms?—I think not; I think the security will be good, but we do not expect to raise anything like 20,000 *l.*

569. How much do you think, practically, of raising?—It would depend again the cost of building vessels a good deal, and we will only do that as we require it; we will not begin to borrow, and then begin to build, but we will see what we are

are going to do, and borrow what will make five vessels, perhaps, or 10 vessels.

570. You will not contemplate an immediate expenditure of more than 15,000 l.?—I do not think it will come to as much as that, but we want to provide for the future.

571. Supposing we take 15,000 l., roughly speaking, as the amount you may want to borrow and expend before you and the public see your way to what the financial consequences to the undertaking will be, is it your conviction that you will be able without difficulty to raise that sum upon moderate terms?—I think so.

572. What rate of interest do you expect to pay for it?—Five per cent.

573. Did I understand you to say that the shareholders have no personal liability?—I understand it is so, but we have never taken an opinion upon it.

574. Is it under the Limited Liability Act?—No, it is not. It was a Company established in 1843, under an Act of Parliament, and there were no limited companies at that time.

575. And there is no personal liability of the shareholders?—No, I think not.

576. Under those circumstances what is the security that you would offer?—We have our own net traffic of 1,200 l. a year as part of the security, and we have the fact that we are paying off gradually the debt we owe to the Board of Works.

577. In fact, your security is the profit of your present undertaking?—Yes, and the expected profits of the new undertaking.

578. That is hardly a security. The only security you have in hand to offer is the value of your own undertaking?—Yes.

579. And you regard that as being sufficient to cover the loan?—We will not get so much. If the property is not considered of sufficient value, we will not be able to borrow.

580. And if you are not able to borrow, the scheme will practically not be carried out?—Yes, it will; we can attend to the traffic when there is water to float the boats.

581. Does not the success of the undertaking, in your own mind, depend upon your being able to raise and to expend this capital sum?—If 10,000 is all that we can necessarily do with. If we cannot get the money, we will allow the owners of the lighters and the other people to have the traffic.

582. Mr. Arthur O'Connor.] You have no lighters, have you?—No, it is only for the purpose of providing a larger traffic that makes us take those clauses; we never spend any more than the 10,000 l.

583. Chairman.] When do you expect to get the 3,500 l., as the works progress?—I do not know; there is nothing said about that.

584. Of course you would not expect it until you have raised the capital that you propose to raise?—I think we would expect it in any case.

585. Is it part of the understanding with the Government that you should begin with their 3,500 l., and spend that before you raise any more?—No, there is no understanding about it; it is a gift.

586. It remains for the Treasury to determine at what time they will make that advance?—Yes.

587. Mr. Arthur O'Connor.] Do you propose to borrow anything from the Board of Works?—If they can give it us.

588. Besides this advance of 3,000 l., you propose to get and borrow?—No, that is not what we propose to do; we propose to let that money go as fair as it will go, and then borrow what is necessary afterwards from the Board of Works, if we can get terms.

589. How much do you propose to borrow from the Board of Works?—About 5,000 l.

590. The balance of the 10,000 l.?—Yes.

591. What is the highest dividend your Company have ever paid?—I think we paid 2 per cent.

592. What did you pay the last year, or last half-year?—One-and-a-quarter per cent.

593. Two years ago it was 1½ per cent, was it not?—Yes.

594. It was 2 per cent. two years ago; then it was 1½ per cent, and the last dividend was 1¼ per cent, was it?—Yes, and the one before that was 1 per cent.

595. So that your canal does not pay so much as it used to pay?—The earnings are larger.

596. But the expenditure is greater?—Yes.

597. How is it, if the earnings are larger and the expenditure not greater, that you have not had a larger dividend?—Because we are carefully keeping our money for a future day.

598. You are making a reserve fund?—No.

599. What is the amount of it?—That is one of the details I could hardly speak to.

600. Could you tell the Committee approximately what it is?——

Mr. *Rea.*] We have not a fixed reserve fund. We have carried forward a larger balance in the last two years than we did previously.

Mr. *Arthur O'Connor.*] The reserve fund consists of the balance; what is the amount of your balance?

Mr. *Rea.*] The balance carried forward last year was 1,270 *l.* 14 *s.* 9 *d.*, and the balance carried forward in the previous year was only 978 *l.*

601. That sum of 1,270 *l.* 14 *s.* 9 *d.* is the largest balance that you have ever had.

Mr. *Rea.*] It is the largest that I recollect.

602. *Chairman* (to the *Witness*).] Have you any reason to expect a loan from the Board of Works?—The Government have been very right in saying that they are not to be asked for a loan. We hope they may change their minds upon that subject, and when they find that the works are going on prosperously, that they will say, " Well, if you want this money, we will give it through the Board of Works."

603. That is an idea in your own mind?—Yes.

604. Have you any reason from anything that has passed between you and the Board of Works to expect that they may take that course?—We have never asked them.

605. Sir *Richard Wyatt.*] In your opinion, will the dividends of the Company be increased if this proposed scheme of amalgamation is carried out?—Yes; we expect that our benefit will be from the increased traffic upon the Lagan Canal.

606. Was that the consideration that actuated the Company in accepting this transfer?—It was.

607. But, in your opinion, it will really lead not only to the better development of the traffic of the district, but also be an advantage to your Company?—Yes; the bulk of the traffic will go through, over our canal.

608. At present your canal is to a certain extent starved by reason of the other system being defective, is it not?—We can hardly say it is starved.

609. It is prejudiced?—It is prejudiced.

610. Mr. *Arthur O'Connor.*] That is to say, if you can get a present of another canal 44 miles long, with land attached to it, which pays rent, or the tenants on which pay rent, you may look for a larger income, and therefore you can increase your dividends?—Yes, of course.

Sir *Richard Wyatt.*] Will the Committee allow me to say that the honourable Member for Belfast, Sir William Ewart, wishes to be relieved; and I propose, with the permission of the Committee, to call him.

Chairman.] I did not understand that you were going to call him.

Sir *Richard Wyatt.*] Yesterday, if the Committee remember, I mentioned that this Bill, being an unopposed Bill so far as Petitions were concerned, of course I was not aware of any question arising with reference to the necessity for this measure. Now question having arisen, it becomes necessary that we should supplement the formal evidence which I intended to offer.

Chairman.] Would you wish to put any further Witness into the Chair except Sir William Ewart?

Sir *Richard Wyatt.*] I have now a gentleman here representing some of the largest freighters in the district, who are very desirous of seeing this Bill carried out; to show the universal feeling in favour of this project being carried out; and that is really the preamble of the Bill.

Chairman.] We promised to examine, and we expect Mr. Jackson, the Secretary to the Treasury, to be here soon, and we shall be bound to put him in the Chair as soon as he comes. Probably Sir William Ewart's examination will not take long.

Sir *Richard Wyatt.*] I will put the matter very generally to Sir William Ewart, so that the Committee will have an opportunity of hearing what the unanimous feeling is with reference to the scheme.

Sir WILLIAM EWART, Bart. (a Member of the House), sworn; and Examined.

611. Sir *Richard Wyatt.*] You are one of the representatives of Belfast?—Yes, I am.

612. And are you aware of the object of this Bill?—Yes.

613. And have you had an opportunity of learning the feeling of the community which you represent with reference to this measure?—Yes, I have had many opportunities of learning it during the last three or four years, and I should say there is only one feeling in Belfast amongst the mercantile classes, or amongst those who understand the matter, in favour of the Bill as one likely to be a great benefit to trade and to the parts of Ireland through which the canal passes.

614. Do you share the opinion which has been almost universally expressed, with reference to the expediency of carrying out this measure?—I am very strongly in favour of the Bill, for the reasons I have already given.

615. *Chairman.*] I presume you have no opinion to express to the Committee upon the question of the cost of the necessary alterations in the canal; the deepening of it?—No, I have no information upon that point.

616. The Company propose to take powers in the Bill to raise an amount not exceeding 20,000 *l.*, to be expended partly in deepening and repairing the canal, and partly upon lighters and expenditure of that kind. Do you think that the Company are in a position to borrow that sum, or a certain proportion of it from the public upon fair terms?—The managers of the Company, or the Company really is composed of very respectable and very able men, and I have every confidence that what they propose to do they will effectually carry out. I have entire confidence in the Company.

617. Mr. *Arthur O'Connor.*] Belfast is a very prosperous and enterprising community, is it not?—Yes.

618. There is plenty of wealth in Belfast; intelligent merchants and men with capital?—Yes.

619. The Lagan Canal connects Belfast with Lough Neagh, does it not?—Yes.

620. Belfast, therefore, is directly interested in the prosperity of the Lagan Canal?—Very much.

621. And any increase of the traffic of the canal would be to the interest of

622. The sum which is necessary, or which it represented as sufficient to put the Ulster Canal in working order, a sum of minus 20,000 l., would be a very small item in comparison with the resources of Belfast, would it not?—Yes.

623. Have any Belfast merchants or other gentlemen ever proposed or contemplated the undertaking themselves as an undertaking likely to be remunerative to those who undertake it?—I have heard of no other rival Company.

624. If this canal was put in working order, at either the public expense or at the expense of third parties, whether the traffic on it was small or great, it would to a certain degree increase the traffic upon the Lagan Canal naturally, would it not?—It would be a feeder.

625. And so benefit the community in Belfast?—Yes.

626. Could you, of your own knowledge, or as the result of your own inquiries, tell the Committee what prospect there is of making that canal a paying concern by itself?—I rely upon the character and the strength of the Company to carry out all that they have proposed.

627. That is to say, you give them your general confidence?—My entire confidence.

628. It is enough for you that this Company has proposed to take it over?—On the terms, certainly; I would not terms upon them that they should not alienate the canal without the consent of Parliament.

629. May I ask whether you would be personally prepared to advance any money, as a shareholder, in the attempt to make the Ulster Canal a paying commercial concern?—I do not go much in for works of that kind, but I think it would afford a fair prospect of good dividend.

630. On its own merits?—Yes.

631. Sir *Richard Wyatt*.] This system, I mean the three canals when united, will really be a system in competition with the Great Northern Railway of Ireland, will it not?—It will.

632. Then I presume that those, on whose behalf you have spoken, would be glad to have what are called two strings to their bow?—No doubt about it. There is an exceedingly strong feeling to that effect.

633. At present the railway company have a monopoly, by reason of the defective state of the Ulster Canal, have they not?—They have.

634. Therefore they are extremely anxious to see this Bill pass in order that they may have two strings to their bow?—No doubt that influences the people of Belfast very much.

635. Mr. *Russell*.] And it would influence any other commercial community in the same way, would it not?—Yes, certainly.

Mr. WILLIAM LAWIES JACKSON (a Member of the House), sworn;
and Examined.

be dependent upon the House of Commons, but that, so far as the Government were concerned, they had no intention of withdrawing from the understanding which had been arrived at between Mr. Hibbert, a former Secretary to the Treasury, and subsequently confirmed or approved by Mr. Fowler, the Secretary of the Treasury, and also by myself in introducing the Estimates of last year; and I think I may say that the Government would deem it right to adhere to the arrangement or understanding which had been come to in former years; and in the event of this Bill being passed (I say this now, although, as I have said, there is no undertaking to that effect), the Government would be prepared to recommend to the House of Commons a vote for this purpose. I understand that the works necessary to put the canal in order will cost a great deal of money, and, as the Committee know the annual cost of maintenance is, I think, about 1,100 l. or 1,200 l. a year to the Government at present, the Government are of opinion that a contribution to that amount would be a satisfactory transaction, in order to get rid of an annual cost of maintenance of about 1,200 l. a year; and at the same time to secure (as I understand the general opinion is that this Bill, if carried, would secure) to the public a canal in good working to prosecution of the works?—There has been no communication addressed to me since I have been at the Treasury upon that question, but I believe that when the arrangement was first come to, and the Government introduced the first Bill, it was contemplated at that time to make a loan of or to spend about 10,000 l., giving them a margin of another 2,000 l.—I think that is in the Bill of 1884. If I remember rightly. I believe that at that time some negociations took place in the direction of the Government making a loan to the Company on favourable terms. I believe that arrangement was subsequently modified by Mr. Hibbert, and took the form of a proposal to make a grant of 3,000 l., and to make a loan, extending over a period of years, I think. I am not quite sure, but I think of 7,000 l. or 9,000 l., but of course, if the Company went to the Board of Works to seek a loan in addition to the grant, that loan, I take it, would be dealt with as any other application for a loan would be dealt with, and would be dealt with upon its merits, and such a loan would only be made on a security which was satisfactory to the Board of Works.

646. Would that be the security of the property of the Lagan Canal?—That, of course, I cannot say until the application is made to them and the security is forthcoming.

647. I think the amount proposed to be granted is 3,500 l.?—Yes.

648. If, besides the out-and-out part of 3,500 l., the Company apply for a Government loan of 7,000 l. or 9,000 l., that will amount to the probable total expenditure, according to the evidence of the chairman of the Company?—I thought you put it at 20,000 l.

649. No; that is the limit of their borrowing powers. The chairman of the Company does not contemplate so large an expenditure; but, however that may be, where would the security of the Government be if the whole of the money was advanced in the way that has been described?—I am not able to speak of the security, because the proposal has never come become before me, and I do not know what security the Company might be prepared to offer. I have known cases where even personal security has been offered in the case of loans which have been applied for to the Government.

650. Mr. Russell.] But you would not grant a loan without good security?—No, certainly not. The loan would be dealt with on its merits in the ordinary business way, and the loan would not be made unless the security was satisfactory to the Board of Works.

651. Chairman.] But as the matter has been put before us, so far it has been presented in this way. An original proposal of a loan of 10,000 l., and objection on the part of Mr. Hibbert, the then Secretary to the Treasury, to that loan, and a counter proposal by him instead of a loan of an out-and-out grant of 3,500 l. Now, if b sides the out-and-out grant of 3,500 l., you are to lend 7,000 l. or 9,000 l., then you will be worse off than under the original proposal?—I do not think so. This is the Bill of 1885, and by Sub-section B. of Section 2, it says: "the Commissioners may undertake to pay to the Company from time to time, on account of the cost of the said works of repair, if executed in a manner approved by the Commissioners, such sums not exceeding in the whole the sum of 10,000 l., out of moneys provided by Parliament, as may be specified in the agreement; provided that the Treasury, if they think it expedient, may authorise the Commissioners to make such payments as aforesaid to an amount not exceeding in the whole 2,000 l. beyond the said limit of 10,000 l." And then the Sub-section (C) specifies the manner in which the repayment shall be made. Sub-section (C) says, "The Company shall undertake to pay to the Commissioners, in consideration for the said transfer and for such payments as aforesaid on account of the said works of repair, an annuity (in this Act referred to as the said annuity), at the rate of 2 l. 14 s. for every 100 l. so paid by the Commissioners aforesaid, and so in proportion for any less sum, for the period of 50 years, commencing at the expiration of three years from the passing of this Act, to be payable by half-yearly payments on every first day of May and first day of November during the said period, the first of such half-yearly payments to be made on whichever of the said days ensues next after the expiration of the said three years."

652. Have

652. Have you got a copy before you of the present year's Bill?—I have.

653. You will find no clauses or sub-sections at all of the nature of those you have just read in the present Bill?—That is quite so. Of course this is a private Bill, and the other was a Government Bill.

654. But there is no reference in this private Bill to any proposed grant or advance by the Treasury?—None whatever; nor was there, I believe, in the Government Bill of last year, but it took the form of an amount being placed upon the Estimates.

655. Not not only is there no mention in this Bill of any intended grant by the Government, or of any possible additional loan by the Government, but under Clause 9 of this Bill, there is a distinct power taken for the Company to raise the whole of the money they may require by a mortgage of their property from the public?—Just so. I should think that that would go to confirm the view that I ventured to express, that in the case of any application for a loan to the Board of Works in Dublin, it would be dealt with upon its merits, and it leaves it open, of course, to the Company to borrow their money in the market where they can borrow it the cheapest.

656. Does not it occur to you that a company coming to Parliament to give them these borrowing powers should seek to exercise those borrowing powers, and having a promise of a grant from the Government that they should not come upon the Government for the whole of the money in the shape of either grant or loan?—I have not said, I think, that it was in contemplation to come upon the Government for the whole of it.

657. But we have it from the chairman of the Company that they propose to make that application?—That, of course, I have not heard.

658. Would you not think it a more fitting thing that a company which, the Committee understood, consists of responsible and eminent men, and with property of their own connected with a wealthy city like Belfast, should go to the public for the raising of the remainder of the necessary amount of the capital?—My own view certainly would be that it would be very desirable that they should borrow the money from the public; but I do not imagine that Parliament would put a clause in a private Bill prohibiting the Company from going to the Government.

659. Mr. *Russell*.] I suppose you give that as a general view?—I do, and I should like to see it much more largely adopted. I may say just in a word that I have looked upon this Bill as being a private Bill necessary to enable the Company to acquire this property. They have no power, as I understand, to enter into any obligation with regard to this property, except by the aid of Parliament, and I have always looked upon it that the terms of the transfer must necessarily be considered when that power had been acquired. I only look upon this Bill as really an enabling Bill, to enable them to take the property, or to enter into an agreement with regard to it.

660. On the whole, I suppose we may take it that you look upon this grant of 8,500 *l.* as a grant in aid of repairs, which will cost at least a sum of 10,000 *l.*; and you think that, in consideration of the fact that this Company is taking over a loss of 1,200 *l.* a year from the Government, that is not too much for the purpose of this Bill?—I certainly think it is a very good bargain for the Treasury if we can get rid of a liability of 1,200 *l.* a year by a payment of 8,500 *l.* down; and I look upon it further as being a good bargain for the Company that they should get a property which has cost so large a sum of money for so small a sum; and I look upon it also as a very good bargain for the public that they should obtain the advantages, which I hope they will obtain, if this canal is put into working order, and is worked as a canal.

661. Mr. *Arthur O'Connor*.] The consideration which moves the Treasury is the desirability of getting rid of an annual charge which they now stand?—I have said that that is a subsidiary consideration with the Treasury. It is an important one I admit.

662. The consideration which will move from the Company to the Treasury, will only be an annual sum in repayment of money advanced?—I do not quite understand the question.

663. What will the Company give to the Treasury in consideration of this transfer, beyond that which merely represents interest and the repayment of the sum to be advanced by the Treasury?—I do not understand that the Company will give anything to the Treasury beyond the relief of the cost of maintenance that is now imposed on the Treasury.

664. That follows the canal?—Yes.

665. But the Company gives no consideration for the transfer?—They give a consideration which I should imagine would be of value to the public undertaking.

666. I mean to the Treasury?—Well, of course, the obligation under which they come by their Bill to maintain and to work this canal would be an obligation of course embodied in the agreement upon the transfer of the property.

667. Beyond the covenant that may be made there would be no consideration:—There is no money consideration.

668. Has the Treasury made any attempt to realize this canal for a money consideration in other quarters?—I believe it was advertised for sale once.

669. Might I ask you if you can say what would be considered a sufficient money consideration by the Treasury for the surrender or transfer of this canal to any party that might offer to purchase it?—The highest price obtainable.

670. Would the Treasury consent to make a transfer of this canal to a third party for such a consideration as 10,000 l. or 5,000 l.?—I should require to have before me, before I could answer that question, a proposal put in a binding form, with sufficient security that it could be carried out, and would be carried out.

671. Supposing a person was prepared to pay 10,000 l. or 5,000 l. in cash, would you take the cash and transfer the canal?—If there were sufficient security to satisfy the Treasury that the canal would be put into working order, and would be maintained as a working canal, of course the Treasury has no leaning towards one customer or one applicant over another, but I believe there is an obligation to maintain the canal. I am not sure that it could be closed.

Sir *Richard Wyatt*.] It was stated yesterday by the secretary that the property had been advertised and put up to auction, but no one bid for it.

Mr. *Arthur O'Connor*.] I quite understood that.

672. (To the *Witness*). Beyond that advertising, has the Treasury made any effort at all to realise this property?—I am not aware of any effort recently. We have had no intimation given to us that there was any possibility of finding a customer for it.

673. The Treasury is now resorting to an Act of Parliament, as it has resorted in previous years to an Act of Parliament, to get rid of the difficulty in connection with this canal; I suppose another Act of Parliament might get rid of any other difficulties there might be in the way. If it be necessary to effect a sale of this canal for a cash payment, would there be any reason why the Treasury should not introduce an Act of Parliament and carry it out?—None whatever, as far as I know.

674. Would the Treasury now be prepared to accept an immediate money payment for this canal?—There is nothing to prevent, so far as I know, any other applicant for the canal to come forward to the Treasury and make a better offer than that which has been put before them.

675. Would the Treasury lay down any conditions if it sold the canal for an immediate money consideration?—I take it they would lay down the conditions that the canal should be put into working order, and maintained and worked as a canal.

676. Has the Treasury itself put the canal in working order?—Well, they have spent a good deal of money upon it from time to time.

677. What, then, becomes of the obligation to maintain the canal in working order?—I do not think I said that there was an obligation to maintain the canal in working order; an obligation upon the Government to do that. I think what I did say was that I was not sure that there was any power to close the

the canal, and to allow it to fall into disrepair, apart from the general advantage of avoiding that if possible.

678. But is in disrepair at the present moment, is it not?—Yes, it is in disrepair. As I have said, there is an annual sum of about 1,200 l. a year, which is spent upon it for the purpose of preventing it falling into entire disrepair.

679. You told us that this annual sum is one of 1,100 l.; could you inform the Committee how that 1,1000 l. is expended?—I can give you one year, which I daresay would show that. This is the Report of the Commissioners of Public Works for the year ending the 31st March 1887.

680. Mr. *Healy*.] What report is that?—This is the annual report of the Board of Works.

681. What page are you referring to?—Page 39; it is an Appendix under the head of " Maintenance and Supplies," there is this expenditure, Ulster Canal, 8 l. 9 s. 0 d.; and then under the heading " Repairs, Fittings, &c., by servants of the Board of Works " 1,065 l. 2 s. 1 d. Then there is " materials used by them," which cost 138 l. 9 s.; " rent and insurance," 4 l. 16 s. 9 d., making a total for that year of 1,216 l. 17 s.

682. In what year was that?—That was the year ending 31st March 1887.

Mr. *Arthur O'Connor*.] That does not appear to include any salaries.

683. Mr. *Healy*.] Are there no lock-keepers here?—Yes, that appears in the Estimates, I think. I beg your pardon; the 1,065 l. 2 s. 1 d. appears under the head of " Pay," and 138 l. 9 s. is the amount of the materials.

684. Then, except the 138 l. 9 s., there is close upon 1,065 l. 2 s. 1 d. for pay?—Yes, it would include workmen.

685. Mr. *Arthur O'Connor*.] How much of that is for wages of workmen employed upon the repairs; and how much for salaries for lock-keepers?—I am afraid I have not got that information.

686. You have to deduct from that the wages of the lock-keepers?—Yes, I am not sure that I can give you the wages of the lock-keepers' salaries, but in the estimates for the current year the salary of the superintendent of the Tyrone Navigation and Ulster Canal is stated to be 241 l. Then the Ulster lock keepers are put in one sum, there are 24 of them, and they apparently receive from four guineas up to 32 l. 10 s. a year; I have not got the total. There are 24 of them, but they are not separated.

687. There is no average shown?—No, I am afraid not.

688. So that of this 1,065 l., more than half goes in salaries?—The lock-keepers would of course include the whole of the lock-keepers on the whole of the navigation which may be under the Board of Works.

689. There are half-a-dozen of them, are there not?—Yes. There is the Shannon.

690. And the Bann?—Yes, and others. I did not mention the Tyrone, but there is a charge for that; and it amounts to 400 l. a year, and there is 3 l. 11 s. for the maintenance and supplies upon the Tyrone navigation.

691. That goes over to the Company?—Gone no.

692. Mr. *Healy*.] Is this in addition to the 1,200 l.?—Yes, in addition to the 1,200 l. which I have referred to.

693. Then you lose 1,200 l. a year?—By the two.

694. Mr. *Russell*.] That makes the bargain still better for the Treasury, does it not?—It makes the position of the Treasury still worse. I will put it in that way.

695. Mr. *Healy*.] How is the 400 l. made up?—It is made up of " Maintenance and Supplies," 3 l. 11 s.; " Pay," 374 l. 18 s. 8 d.; " Materials used, 16 l. 17 s. 11 d.; " Fuel, Light, Water, and Cleaning," 7 l. 16 s.; making total of 401 l. 17 s. 2 d.

696. Colonel *Saunderson*.] That pay is not all to lock-keepers but to labourers employed upon the canal, is it not?—It would include everything that comes under the heading of pay.

697. Mr. *Arthur O'Connor.*] That is to say, a canal of about four miles in length costs about 100 *l.* a mile or 80 *l.* a mile, and the Ulster Canal, of 44 miles long, has, instead of 874 *l.* spent in repairs, 1,000 *l.* ; that is three times as much, although it is ten times the length ?— Yes, of course ; I have not the details, nor could I say positively whether the 400 *l.* expended in that year upon the Tyrone is the average amount. I have not verified that.

698. Now, with regard to the superintendent, who receives 240 *l.* a year, What do the Government contemplate doing with him, and how does he hold his post ?—I am afraid I cannot answer that question.

699. How long has he been in the service ?—I think his name is Mr. Adams, if I remember rightly, and I think he has a service of more than 40 years upon the Board of Works ; but I think he has probably arrived at that period of life when a little rest might be requisite.

700. Mr. *Healy.*] I suppose he has promoted this Bill, too ?—I have no knowledge of that.

701. Mr. *Arthur O'Connor.*] Is he to be transferred with the canal ?—I should think not, but I cannot answer that question.

702. If he is not, the charge in respect of his salary or his pension will continue on the Treasury, will it not ?—That would continue in any case.

703. Then you do not get rid of part of the charge, even if you transfer the canal ?—I think it could hardly be expected that, in the case of a man who had given 40 years of his service his pension would be withheld by the Treasury, if he is entitled to one.

704. Is it a fact, even if this transfer takes place, that the suggested reduction of the Estimates by the total sum mentioned will not take place, inasmuch as this man's salary at any rate, or his pension, will remain an imperial charge ?—I think he has given some period of his total service to this canal, but I believe that previously to that he was engaged by the Board of Works otherwise.

705. Is there anybody else connected with either the Tyrone or the Ulster Navigation in a similar position ?—I am not able to say.

706. You are not able to say there are not ?—Of course, if you push the argument very far you might say that the whole of the Office of Works in Dublin is more or less engaged upon work in connection with this, in superintendence, and so on.

707. What I want to ascertain is whether there will not be a very substantial reduction of the Estimates ; at any rate, with reference to one item it appears that there will not be a reduction ?—Of course, I can only offer an opinion upon that, because I have not the facts before me ; but I should incline to the opinion that inasmuch as a possible transfer of this property has been within the contemplation of the Government, and of the Board of Works, for at least four years, the expenditure on the repairs during that period of four years would naturally, I think, be kept down to the minimum ; and, therefore, if a transfer is not made it might be, as I say I have not the facts, but it might be that the expenditure in succeeding years might even be larger than the average of the past.

708. And it might be less. You say that the Treasury has entered into an undertaking to make any grant to the Lagan Company ?—That is so.

709. But then you consider it a point of honour not to depart from the position taken up by your predecessors ?—That is so.

710. But that, at any rate, the grant is to be advanced only, *pari passu*, with the completion of, at any rate, the first portion of the works ?—Certainly, that is my understanding of it.

711. At the same time, as we have heard, it is contemplated, at any rate, by the Company to come to the Board of Works for a sum of some 6,000 *l.* to be advanced upon loan, in order to put them in funds to complete the work ?—Yes, the chairman has said so.

712. Now, do you consider that the check of the Board of Works in respect of the advance of 3,500 *l.* from time to time, as the work is completed, is anything more than illusory, when with the other hand you are advancing

the amount of money to the same company?—I do not look upon the check of the Board of Works as being illusory. On the contrary, I should expect that the Board of Works would not make the advance, would not pay over the money or the instalments, if I may use that term, except upon proof and satisfaction to them that work to that value had been done; and I think that would be a complete check, in far as the expenditure of the money went.

713. Now I ask your attention to Section 5 of the Bill. You see there provision is made for extending the borrowing powers of the Company, and that the sum borrowed may be expended on the following purposes, or any of them: "1. For giving the Ulster Canal a navigable depth of five feet, at least, from end to end, and otherwise improving the works thereof. 2. For the purpose of providing, by building or purchase, vessels, animals, and apparatus for the purpose of the carriage and hauling upon the said canals. 3. For the purpose of subscribing to any company or association for carrying goods upon the said canals. And 4. For the purpose of subscribing to any company or association making or managing any tramway connected with the said canals, or any part or parts thereof." There is no binding obligation upon the Company to expend any money borrowed upon any one of those four objects in particular; that it will be at liberty to appropriate the money borrowed by any one of the four to the exclusion of the other three?—Yes, no doubt it would be possible to do that.

714. Therefore the Company may advance the money "for the purpose of subscribing to any company or association for carrying goods upon the said canals"?—Certainly.

715. Are you aware that the Canal Company itself does not own any lighters?—I have no knowledge upon that.

716. Are you aware that the secretary of the Company in his private capacity is the owner of lighters working upon the canal?—No, I do not know it.

717. Do you see anything in that clause that would prevent the Company, after obtaining money upon loan in its corporate capacity, from subscribing to the private undertaking of its own secretary?—I am afraid that is rather a legal question, and I should not like to offer any opinion upon it.

718. Has the Treasury contemplated that state of things?—I do not think it is a matter that concerns the Treasury.

719. It did not enter into the contemplation of the Treasury in forming an estimate of the merits of the proposal?—Not in the least. This is a power which the Company asks Parliament to give them; to borrow a sum of money, not exceeding 30,000 L., for certain purposes; but if Parliament entrusts the Company with those powers, and if the money is not borrowed from the Treasury, I should not deem the Treasury to be concerned.

720. But Parliament does not propose to give the Company these powers without knowing the facts of the case?—That is a matter for the Committee and not for me, I think.

721. And it is also the duty of the Treasury, is it not, to inquire into the facts of the case?—I do not see the connection myself.

722. Mr. Healy.] In the event of the Company failing to carry out the canal if they find it a bad speculation, what is to become of the canal then?—I think it reverts, so far as I remember.

723. It reverts to the Board of Public Works?—Yes.

724. And supposing in three years time they find this a bad speculation, they will have had 3,600 L. from you, and you will have all this thing over again?—They will then have had the money which will have been expended upon the canal, and presumably the canal would be the better for the expenditure.

725. And you will have the trouble all over again?—I hope not.

726. Is there anything to show that all this trouble will not begin again as soon as they find they have made a bad bargain, and drop the thing like a hot potato?—I think it is contemplated that in addition to the grant which Parliament might give them they would expend other moneys, and I certainly should think that the canal would not be in a worse but in a better position at that time.

727. What security will the country have that in two or three years time, when these gentlemen, finding that they have made a bad bargain, that they will not throw the thing upon your hands again?—If they were unable to carry out their obligation, of course we should revert practically to the position that we are in to-day; we should be in no worse position.

728. Would you re-appoint your superintendent at 241 l. a year?—I think it has been stated that the superintendent has a long period of service; and probably if we keep the canal we shall have to appoint somebody else in his place.

729. Has the question of the leasing, instead of granting, been considered by the Treasury?—Yes, it has been considered; that is to say, I have considered it. There has been no negotiation, I think; but it was a suggestion which rather occurred to me, with a view of avoiding the difficulties which had been experienced in passing the Bill through Parliament, and I did ask the question whether we had not the power to lease the canal to them; but after consideration I do not see that really any advantage could be obtained, because the lease would not relieve us of the obligation in case they failed to take it back again.

730. Has any effort been made by the Board of Works taking the four miles of the Tyrone Navigation to reduce this charge of 400 l. or 100 l. a mile?—I am afraid I cannot give a very definite answer to that. It is their duty, of course, to keep down the expenditure to the very lowest point.

731. Considering that there are no lighters upon the canal, and the locks cannot be numerous, can you arrive at any reasonable conclusion why a four-mile canal should cost 400 l. for maintenance?—I am afraid I cannot answer that question, because I do not know the number of locks, and I do not know the details of the expenditure.

732. Are you aware the secretary said that in the event of the navigation of the Bann being abolished, and is being allowed to run as God intended it should, and used for drainage purposes, they consider that they would have a claim for compensation in case that navigation was interfered with?—No.

733. Would you think it a reasonable thing that a clause should be inserted in this Bill that the operation of the drainage works in Lough Neagh and the Lower Bann should give them no claim for compensation?—I am afraid I should not like to express an opinion upon that; I am not sufficiently conversant with the district and the possibilities.

734. Do you think it a reasonable thing to give these people who are getting this bargain, upon which the country has spent 300,000 l., a vested interest in possible future expenditure by reason of future works upon the Lower Bann?—As I say, I do not understand the point, and therefore I would rather not give an opinion upon it.

735. Would you think it a reasonable thing to prevent their having such a right to make such a claim?—I think probably the general law would have to apply with reference to such a case.

736. You think it will turn out a good speculation, even taking that into consideration?—I hope it will.

737. As I understand, you are going to pension off the superintendent; in case the Company turn off all the lock-keepers and labourers, and so on, will not they have no charge upon the rates, or will any guarantee be taken with regard to the discharge of these local men?—I am not aware that the question has been raised, but I can say that of course there is a great difference between pledging yourself by a clause in an Act of Parliament that you will not turn off a man, and turning a man off without such a pledge.

738. Once you part with your contract, what power will you have to prevent hardships?—Once a Clause is inserted in the Act of Parliament, the Company will not have it in their control to take any other course.

739. But the Treasury would?—But I think it would be a very unusual Clause to insert in an Act of Parliament to say, you, the Company, shall, so long as this man lives, not even subject to good behaviour, continue to pay his wages.

740. But you are going to pension the man who has been in receipt of 241 l.

a year, and the other man is to be left to the mercy of the elements?—It is not a question of being left to the mercy of the elements, because it is not a condition of employment you can enforce; a man, presumably, enters the service at a lower rate of payment if he is entitled to a pension.

741. Will you tell the Committee why the Bill, instead of merely handing over the water-way to the Company, hand it over on condition of the payment of 120 *l.* or 130 *l.* a year?—It hands over the whole of the property, and the transaction must be looked at as a whole.

742. That would be of the actual value of 130 *l.* a year?—Of course, it would depend partly upon whether it was a payment secured, or whether it was subject to abatements.

743. There is an actual rental now from the canal of 130 *l.*, and you are proposing to give that away as an absolute gift?—I think you may take it, and I do not hesitate to express, as I have already expressed, that I think the Company got a very good bargain.

744. I will take it in this way. Supposing that you were offered 1,000 *l.* for this rental, would you think that a fair thing without the canal?—I think we could not separate it. Probably there are some way-leaves necessary.

745. Precisely; but why is the Company not merely given the water-way, which they say is all they want, or which the local public say is all they want; but why should not this go in ease of local taxation?—The answer to that is that this is the best arrangement which hitherto the Treasury has been able to make.

746. Supposing you offered the Canal to the Company and any way-leaves they wanted, and you kept the rental in your own possession if you did not want the 1,000 *l.*, why should it not go in ease of local taxation?—I think probably the Company would say, we have taken into account the whole of the property as it stands, including the rentals; we are going to enter into obligations that will impose upon us a considerable charge and responsibility, and this is one of the conditions upon which we enter upon those terms.

747. Do you think it reasonable that as the Government are now parting with their control over this canal, and handing it into private people's hands, the Grand Juries and Boards of Guardians and other persons interested should have some representation upon the directorate, or that the Board of Works should be able to nominate some such persons?—I am not very much in favour of official directors; I should say that the interests of the public would be more likely to be served by making it to the interests of the Company to obtain the largest revenue, which means giving the best service to the public which they could.

748. When this Bill passes, you wash your hands completely of this thing, and may get it back again for anything you know, in a state of absolute

on its merits as Bills of the kind usually are, and that they would be entitled, out of the funds of the Company, to pay the legitimate costs of the application.

752. Mr. *Arthur O'Connor.*] In case this Lagan Company takes over the canal, the committee of management are to be called the " board of directors of the Company, and the Lagan Navigation Act, 1843, and the Lagan Navigation Act, 1873, shall be read as if in the sections of the said Acts relating to the committee of management, the board of directors were referred to in lieu of the said committee, and the said Acts shall have effect accordingly." What I want to ask you is this: Whether there is anything in the Act of 1843 or in the amending Act of 1873, or in this Act, to compel the Lagan Company to maintain the canal as a going concern; whether there is any power resident in the Board of Works, or in the Treasury, or anywhere else, to take them to task if they simply abandon the canal or use the land of it for any other purpose?—There is, of course, a limitation of the power of the Company in Clause 7, that they " shall not sell, lease, or otherwise dispose of the said canals or either of them, or of any land or property held on account thereof, without the sanction of the Commissioners in writing having previously been obtained.

753. But where is the provision for reverter?—It is in Sub-section B. of Clause 3, which says: " The Company shall keep the said canals open for navigation and in a fit state of repair, and provision may be made for the forfeiture of the said canals by the Company, and the reverter thereof to the Commissioners on default being made by the Company in such undertaking," and I imagine that the agreement would contain a clause to carry that out.

754. If that were carried out after the Lagan Company had neglected the canal and got it into a thorough state of disrepair, what possible inducement could there be for the Board of Works to resume, under the provisions of this section, an admittedly embarrassing asset, which has only cost them, up to the present time, an annual outlay of 1,100 *l.* or 1,200 *l.*?—I cannot imagine this Company taking over the canal at all, if it was in their contemplation to allow it to fall into disrepair. I cannot imagine that the Company can get any benefit out of the canal, except by having it put in order and working it.

755. Surely it is a benefit to the Lagan Company to take over this land which is now in the occupation of tenants and for which rent is paid?—It only brings in 150 *l.* a year.

756. But the Lagan Company itself is not a very large one, is it?—I take it that the Lagan Company would look rather to this as a feeder, which would benefit them just as a railway company benefits by sometimes taking over a branch line which by itself does not pay, but which brings traffic on to the main line, out of which they get their profits.

757. Are you aware that the Committee of 1881 reported that there was a considerable amount of land which was fit for grazing, and that there was a considerable amount of land which was fit for tillage?—Yes, I believe that is so.

758. Is not that a valuable property of itself?—I think it is. I have said several times that I think it is an exceedingly good bargain for the Company.

759. Now, with regard to the men who are employed about this canal, they are at present the servants of the Board of Works, are they not?—Yes, of course they may be in temporary pay.

760. Do the Board of Works claim that in respect of all these people they are entitled to hand them over to the service of a private company?—I do not think there would be any difficulty about any friendly arrangement being arrived at between the two.

Company to secure that these workmen should not suffer, as far as it can be done.

762. But does the Treasury, by any covenant in the agreement, secure themselves against any claim on the part of the existing servants of the Board of Works?—No.

763. Has the Treasury caused any estimate to be made of the capital sum which would be represented by such possible claims?—I cannot conceive such claims arising.

764. Take the case of the officer to be superannuated, the superintendent, that represents a certain capital sum, does it not?—Of course the officer, if he were superannuated, would receive a pension what he is entitled to, as at present. His position is not, I mean, affected by this Bill.

765. But, with regard to the others, what do you say?—I suppose these lockkeepers are men on weekly wages, most of them.

766. The Treasury has not made any estimate or caused any inquiry to be made with reference to the amount of claims that might be put forward with reference to these servants?—No. If the Bill is passed, if Parliament gives the Company its Bill, and I hope they will get it, of course then it will be the duty of the Board of Works to enter into relations with the Company to settle an agreement; and it would be a very proper thing for them to consider between the Company and the Board of Works which of the men could be taken over by the Company; and I should hope that the Company would meet them in a fair spirit and take over all the men who were useful to them.

Mr. THOMAS SEXTON (a Member of the House), sworn; and Examined.

767. Sir Richard Wyatt.] You are Lord Mayor of Dublin?—Yes.

768. And one of the Representatives of Belfast?—Yes, West Belfast.

769. In the latter capacity you have had an opportunity of learning the views of your constituents with reference to the desirability of this Bill receiving the sanction of Parliament, had you not?—Yes; of my constituents, and generally of the people of the province of Ulster.

770. I do not think you were in the room when Sir William Ewart gave his evidence, but I put this question to him; at present the Great Northern Railway Company have practically the monopoly of the traffic through the district traversed by the canal system, have they not?—They have.

771. Is it your opinion that if this Bill passes and the three canal companies are united and worked as one in the improved condition contemplated, namely, the lowering of the water of the Ulster Canal, that will enable the Canal Company to compete with the railway?—I think that result would certainly follow.

772-3. And is it the opinion of your constituents as far as you have been able to ascertain it, as well as your own, that it is highly desirable that they should have the advantage of the competition thus offered to the traders of the locality?—I believe it is, and I may add that this Bill is the only legislative matter in regard to which, as being one of the Members of Belfast, I find all kinds of people in Belfast agreeing.

774. Are you aware of any organised opposition to this measure, are you aware that public meetings have been held?—I have observed the course of public opinion, and I am not aware of any article in a newspaper, or of any resolution of a public body, or of any resolution of a public meeting in opposition to the Bill.

775. Mr. Russell.] The remark you apply to all classes of people in Belfast, with regard to their being in favour of this Bill. I suppose you apply to all classes in Ulster, at least to those that will be affected by the canal?—Yes, the expressions of public opinion in the district affected by the canal have been uniform, and without any exception, in favour of the Bill. I believe the great majority of them are in favour of the Bill.

776. Have you paid any attention to the conditions the Company have made

made with reference to the objections that have been taken to the Bill?—Yes, I have paid some attention to them.

777. Do you consider them satisfactory, or otherwise?—I should not like to give an absolutely positive reply upon that point.

778. You did not hear the secretary's evidence yesterday?—No.

779. Chairman.] Do you know anything of the question which has been started here of a possible scheme for lowering the level of Lough Neagh? Yes.

779.* Do you regard that as a probable feature of the scheme that will be likely to be affected?—I regard that question as one to be dealt with by scientific opinion rather than by any opinion I can express upon the matter.

780. Are you aware, or is it within your knowledge, that if Lough Neagh were lowered below what is called the summer level, those canals would become useless without their level being further lowered?—I have heard it maintained that if the lake were lowered below the summer level, the effect would be injurious to the canal, but I have also heard it maintained that it will not be necessary for any navigation works in another quarter to lower the lake below the summer level.

781. Is not one of the objects of lowering the level of the Lough to free certain rich bordering lands from being rapidly overflowed?—Yes, certainly.

782. And for that purpose it might be necessary to lower the level of the Lough Neagh below the summer level?—Yes, possibly. There are two opinions upon the subject, and I cannot pretend to decide between them.

783. Mr. Russell.] May I ask you whether you are aware that the damage to those lands on the sides of the Bann arises from the lake when it is above the summer level?—Yes. As I have tried to convey to the Committee, that is one of the contentions; in fact, it is identical with the contention that no damage is done in the lake with respect to the summer level.

784. Chairman.] Supposing that we wished to ascertain for our own satisfaction that the scheme of lowering the level of Lough Neagh for those purposes would not involve lowering it below the summer level, could you satisfy the Committee upon that point, or must we refer to some other evidence?—I could not undertake to satisfy you upon that point.

785. Sir Richard Wyatt.] Of course, if anyone took upon themselves to interfere with the level of Lough Neagh, and to destroy the canal system of the district, they would entail upon themselves a great responsibility and liability to compensation?—That is a speculative question which depends upon circumstances that may arise hereafter.

786. No one would be advised to do that without the sanction of Parliament; nothing short of Parliamentary powers would enable anyone to interfere with the level of Lough Neagh?—The answer to that question depends upon a more extensive knowledge of the law than either than I comprehend to possess.

787. Assuming that to be so, that they would entail upon themselves great liability, that is really the protection against interference with the level of the water?—It I understand you to mean that it would be necessary for any persons, in order to inflict damage by lowering the level, to come to Parliament for that purpose hereafter, I think that would be the proper time when the question of compensation should be raised and considered.

788. And if they did it without the sanction of Parliament, they would incur great responsibility, which alone would be the protection?—Of course, if any one breaks the law, he incurs a responsibility.

Mr. JEREMIAH JORDAN (a Member of the House), sworn; and Examined.

789. Sir Richard Wyatt.] You have heard the evidence of my Lord Mayor of Dublin, and also of Sir William Ewart, I think?—Yes.

790. I think you are interested in a commercial way in this question?—Yes.

791. Do you endorse their views with reference to the desirability of carrying out the scheme contemplated by this Bill?—Yes, and I feel more strongly than they do, in relation to the desirability of having it open as another means of transit for the transmission of goods other than the Great Northern Railway.

792. Have you heard of any organised or individual opposition to the measure in your district?—Not the slightest; all the other way.

793. Mr. *Russell.*] What I wish specially to ask you is this: you have some knowledge, have you not, of the flooding of the lands by the rising of the Lough Erne?—Yes; we have considerable flooding of the land by the rising of the Lough Erne.

794. Does any damage arise when the lake is at the summer level?—Never.

795. The damage arises when the lake is above the summer level?—Always.

796. And not when it is at the summer level? —No, never when it is at the summer level.   In Lough Erne we have very low-lying lands besides the Lough.

797. Are you able to say that the damage arises from Lough Neagh in the same way?—No, I am not able to say.

798. Mr. *Arthur O'Connor.*] Are there not at least 20 loughs between Lough Erne and Lough Neagh?—I am not aware.

799. There are a number of loughs at any rate?—Yes.

800. And the levels of the two loughs are not the same, the level of Lough Neagh and the level of Lough Erne would not be the same in the same work?—I am not able to say that.

801. They are not in the same catchment basin, are they?—No.

802. And the slopes of Lough Erne are not the same as the slopes of Lough Neagh?—No.

803. So that the condition of Lough Erne has nothing to say to the condition of Lough Neagh?—No; but the circumstances might be analogous.

804. No doubt, but is there a thing corresponding with Toome Weir of Lough Erne?—I do not know.

805. Does not the level of Lough Neagh depend upon Toome Weir?—I do not know.

806. Surely Toome Weir is at the mouth of the exit from Lough Neagh down the Lower Bann?—I am not conversant with that district.

807. Now, with regard to the interest in the locality, I think you are from Enniskillen?—Yes.

808. You are commercially interested in Enniskillen?—Yes.

809. And if the canal were opened between Lough Erne and Lough Neagh the commercial community of Enniskillen, at least, in so far as they are in the position of yourself, would have an advantage?—I do not think the commercial community would have an advantage.   It is the consumers in the locality who would have an advantage.   So far as the commercial community is concerned, it makes a very little difference whether we pay ten shillings a ton or fifteen shillings a ton for carriage.   It all goes to the advantage of the consumer, and we apprehend that there would go to the advantage of the consumer something like threepence per week upon Indian meal, or threepence per week upon flour.

810. And you say it is a matter of indifference to the commercial community? —Not wholly indifferent, because we would rather pay, say 10 *l.* upon carriage rather than 15 *l.*, but so far as making money out of the ......, we would make no money; we would have less capital in the carriage, but we would make no money out of the carriage.

811. But you would have to pay for carriage if this canal were opened?— We have a short, competing railway with the Great Northern at present from Sligo to Enniskillen, and we save by that competing railway two shillings a ton ... The carriage of flour, and four shillings in the carriage of American bacon from Liverpool, and we save something like three or four shillings a ton on the carriage of sugar, all by means of that competition line.   It is understood that the Great Northern Railway Company of Ireland will purchase the line, in order to put it out of the way, and then we would have no competing line but the Great Northern to all that part of the country, except we got this Ulster

Canal, and we want the Ulster Canal as a competing line, as against the monopoly of the Great Northern Railway, for the benefit of the community, and not the traders.

812. Have the traders or the community of Enniskillen, any more than the traders or community of Belfast, ever contemplated a commercial undertaking and starting this canal at their own expense?—Never; any more than they have contemplated the undertaking of the Londonderry and Enniskillen Railway, because we have not a penny in it.

813. It is of course only natural that the commercial community in Enniskillen should be glad to see this canal opened?—I think so.

814. In fact you would be lunatics if you were not glad?—Yes.

815. Colonel Saunderson.] Is it not the case that one of the reasons why the population dwelling upon the banks of the canal are so anxious that the Bill should pass, is that the supplies of turf have lately fallen off to a considerable extent, and that the people depend upon the supply of coal, and that the supply of coal is entirely in the hands of the Great Northern Company, who charge a very high price for it, and that, therefore, the people along the banks of the canal hope to get coal at a much cheaper rate?—We are getting coal fairly cheap now by the connection of the Sligo Railway, but if that were closed up we should require to depend entirely upon the Ulster Canal to get coal cheaper.

816. Mr. Arthur O'Connor.] As a matter of fact, you do not now get your coal from the Great Northern Railway?—No. Would you permit me to say, at the same time, in our part of the country we think that the property being there as a canal should not at present be dismantled; and if you will permit me to say, as a public man, I think it is not the time to dismantle any water way or road in Ireland, as, in our part of the country at least, we expect it will be more prosperous, and that there will be a greater population. The canal is there, at any rate, but it is now losing 1,200 l. a year; and we think that if the outlay that is contemplated be made upon it, and that it is still not to be used as a water way, it cannot be in any worse condition than it is at the present time as a losing concern; and the Government cannot be any worse off than they are now, and we consider that the Government have made a very good bargain in paying down the money; and we would advocate that under no circumstances should the canal be dismantled; but, in order to maintain it as a roadway, we would like something like the following conditions: That this company should neither lease, nor let, nor sell, either the land or the canal to any company whatever. We would also like, in order to attain our end, that the traffic should be maintained so long as the company holds the canal, that is, that they should run the lighters upon it; that they should not hold it in their hands, and not use it; and that failing to maintain the traffic, or in case of bankruptcy, the canal should revert to the Commissioners of Works.

817. Mr. Russell.] That is provided for in the Bill?—Yes, so as to maintain the waterway intact.

818. Mr. Arthur O'Connor.] That is not provided for?—No; and that the sum of 8,500 l., and the loans under the Bill, be expended solely on, or in connection with, the canal traffic, and that the existing losses should be maintained, and no compensation be sought for the reduction of Lough Neagh to a low summer level. These are some of the conditions that we would like to be embodied either in the Bill or in an agreement between the Treasury and the Company.

MR. HENRY WILSON sworn, and Examined.

819. Sir Richard Wyatt.] Are you here to represent the firms of John Stevenson and Company, Limited, and the Ream Spinning Company?—Yes.

820. And are those two companies two of the largest freighters upon the canal?—They are.

821. You know what is contemplated by this Bill, I believe?—I do.

822. Do you believe that it would be a great local as well as public advantage that the Bill should pass?—Yes, I believe so.

823. Do you think that if the navigations are improved, as proposed by this Bill, particularly the Ulster Canal, it would be enabled to compete with the Great Northern Railway of Ireland?—Certainly.

824. And is it your desire, and those whom you represent, that they should have the advantage of the two systems of transit?—Certainly.

825. To what extent can you speak with regard to the feelings of other traders upon the canal?—I know that the general feeling in the County Tyrone is strongly in favour of it.

826. And you are aware that public meetings have been held upon the subject?—Yes.

827. Have you heard any opposition from any quarter whatever to the proposed scheme?—Not with the proper safeguards that there seems to be contained in the Bill.

828. You know the provisions of the Bill, and you are here to support them?—Yes.

829. Mr. Russell.] In addition to representing these firms, you represent the lessees at Coalisland, do you not?—Yes.

830. Are you satisfied with the arrangements entered into yesterday by the Secretary?—Yes.

831. Mr. Arthur O'Connor.] You represent two commercial firms, I understand?—Yes.

832. And it would be to the advantage of those two commercial firms that this canal should be open to the traders?—Decidedly; if it closed, Coalisland might close.

833. With regard to three meetings which were held, did you attend them?—Yes, I have attended some meetings.

834. How many meetings did you attend?—Only two meetings in our own neighbourhood.

835. Were you instrumental in getting one meeting up?—I was not.

836. They are included in that little report which was circulated by the reporter in favour of the Bill, are they not?—I do not know; I have not seen it.

837. Mr. Russell.] I suppose generally the people who are interested in the subjects get up the meetings and attend them?—I think so.

The Committee Room was cleared.

After a short time the parties were called in.

Chairman.] The question I desire to put to the parties representing the Company on this occasion is this: We have heard something rather vague of the possibilities of a scheme for lowering the level of Lough Neagh, and we have some reason to suppose that if it were lowered there might be a claim for compensation on the part of the owners of the Ulster Canal. Under the Bill as it is drawn, if the navigation were not kept free the consequence to the Company would be that the canal would be forfeited, and would revert to the Commissioners; and if in the meantime they had only expended the money given or borrowed from the Government they would have incurred no expenditure of their own, and they would be quit, if I read the Bill correctly, by the forfeiture of this canal, but they might still have a claim to compensation in respect of damage to the canal from the lowering of Lough Neagh. How would you propose to meet that consideration.

Sir Richard Wyatt.] I presume that this Committee would not in a private Bill deprive the Company of its rights to seek compensation for any damage done to their property.

Mr. Healy.] We do not touch the Lagan Canal at all.

Sir Richard Wyatt.] Quite so. Then this will be an integral part of the system. When it is amalgamated it will, to all intents and purposes, be a part

0.768.   O 3

of the property of the Lagan Canal Company, and therefore it would be so serious a matter that it would be impossible for them here instructing me to consent to the insertion in a private Bill of an alteration of the general law, whereby they would get compensation if any wilful damage was done to their property.

Chairman.] That I can quite understand; but the question is what should be done with that compensation. Supposing that event happened, and that the Company were to get that compensation; if they were simply to surrender the canal and pocket the compensation, that would not be a legitimate conclusion of this business.

Sir Richard Wyatt.] Will you forgive me, Sir, for asking why not? If a company, or an individual, is damaged by some other body and persons, and they are entitled to compensation, there is always a provision made for the distribution of that compensation amongst the persons particularly damaged, namely, in this case the shareholders. You are aware, Sir, it frequently happens that where property is taken from a company, there is not at this moment in my eye; a large cemetery company.

Mr. Healy.] But this is not your property.

Sir Richard Wyatt.] But it will become our property in consideration of the obligations which we take upon ourselves.

Chairman.] Then I will put it to you in another way, Sir Richard. At present this canal is the property of the Government for the public.

Sir Richard Wyatt.] Yes.

Chairman.] And though at present it is a losing concern, if it were to be damaged in this way the public would get their compensation; is not that so. The compensation would go to the owners of the canal, would it not?

Sir Richard Wyatt.] Yes.

Chairman.] At present the public are the owners of the canal?

Sir Richard Wyatt.] Yes.

Chairman.] And they would get the compensation?

Sir Richard Wyatt.] Yes.

Chairman.] What I want you to address your mind to is this. Under that hypothesis of the lowering of Lough Neagh, and compensation being demanded and obtained by the Company, as far as I at present understand the Bill, they could relieve themselves of their liability to the Government by throwing up the canal, and they could retain possession of the compensation.

Sir Richard Wyatt.] The Government?

Chairman.] No, the Company.

Sir Richard Wyatt.] Well, the transfer is to be upon the usual terms. The Company take all the obligations, and they are to enjoy all the advantages, if any, accruing to the transferors. That, Sir, is an every day contract, as you know, in Parliament. Then if the Government transfer this white elephant to the Lagan Company, and they are willing to take it, if some new law should be passed whereby the property should be destroyed, I apprehend that any legislation upon the subject would provide for compensation, and the application of that money.

Mr. Arthur O'Connor.] The Lagan Company would remain discharged from any liability in respect of the Ulster Canal.

Sir Richard Wyatt.] Yes, but unfortunately they would have been ruined, so to speak, because their property would have suffered in common with the others; and therefore you see, Sir, it would be a calamity to them, and the compensation could not exceed, if was equal to, the loss which they would sustain.

Mr. *Healy.*] Take it the other way. Supposing at the present moment there was a scheme of enormous value to the city of the counties of Derry and of Antrim, to which there were many obstacles, and you proposed to raise up an additional obstacle to the opening of the locks of the Lower Bann by handing over this undertaking as an asset to your Company, do you think it would be a reasonable thing for us to insist that we should not allow such an obstacle to be raised by creating a vested interest in you, by passing a Bill without some guarantee that you will not claim that compensation?

Sir *Richard Wyatt.*] My answer is, that it is not proposed by the Bill to do so.

Chairman.] Will you tell me this? You see the position of the Company in any further contingency would partly depend upon the shape in which this Bill passes as an Act, and partly upon the agreement entered into under it. Now suppose that the event which we are now supposing were to happen, and that the canal was to become unnavigable, the Company would then return the canal upon the hands of the Commissioners. Supposing in the meantime they borrowed money from the Board of Works, what is your expectation, that they would remain liable for the repayment of that sum or that the forfeiture of the canal would acquit them of that liability.

Sir *Richard Wyatt.*] I cannot imagine for a moment, as a draughtsman, that any agreement prepared under this Act of Parliament would not provide for such a contingency.

Chairman.] Then you quite accept the prospect in this eventuality, of the Company remaining liable for any money which they might have succeeded in borrowing from the Government.

Sir *Richard Wyatt.*] No doubt the Government would take care of that.

Mr. *Russell.*] The real question seems to me to be this: You are taking over this property from the Government. Mr. Healy points out that there is something in the air which may lower Lough Neagh below the summer level, and destroy not only this canal, but other canals in Ulster as well, and that by giving you this to-day we may be raising up rights to compensation that we ought not to raise up. Now, have you any evidence, first of all, to show that the damage that Mr. Healy speaks of on the banks of the Bann and which everybody is in favour of remedying, arises not from the summer level of Lough Neagh, but from Lough Neagh when it is at a much higher level than the summer levels, or have you run any evidence that it is proposed to lower Lough Neagh below the summer level, so that this damage will be caused.

Sir *Richard Wyatt.*] I am not aware of what is in the air, as you express it; but all I can say is that, if the Bill should be passed, we hope we shall have the assistance of yourselves and other honourable Members to protect us against any such a calamity. As representing the Company only, and this being a private Bill, I do not think I should be justified in tying the hands in any way of the Government, who are to be one of the contracting parties. This is simply a Bill to enable this agreement to be carried out. I think the proper course and the only course we could very well act upon, or that we could be any parties to, would be a recommendation from the Committee to enable us to make a special Report upon this Bill, that they should suggest that any agreement entered into in pursuance of that should receive the attention of the Government on this point. I need hardly tell honourable Members, particularly the Right honourable Chairman, that it is not an uncommon thing for a Committee to make a recommendation to the Government, but not to enact that their hands should be tied.

Chairman.] I think that is worth considering at any rate.

The Committee Room was cleared.

After a short time the parties were again called in.

Chairman.] The Committee have passed the Preamble of the Bill.

Tuesday, 10th June 1884.

MEMBERS PRESENT:

Mr. Raley.
Mr. Macartney.
Mr. Arthur O'Connor.

Mr. Russell.
Colonel Saunderson.
Mr. Stansfeld.

MR. ARTHUR O'CONNOR, IN THE CHAIR.

The Committee Room was cleared.

After a time the parties were called in.

MR. WILLIAM ROBERT REA, re-called ; and further Examined.

838. *Mr. Russell.*) WILL you turn to Clause 4 of this Bill, sub-section 2, and read it ?—" The Company may take remuneration for such carriage and hauling, so that the rates in respect of the carriage be approved in writing by the Commissioners, and so that the rate for any purpose mentioned in the Lagan Navigation Act, 1873, do not exceed the rate authorised for the purpose by that Act." Does that mean that the rates on the Ulster Canal and Tyrone Navigation are to be the same as the Lagan Navigation ?—So I take it.

839. What are the rates upon the Lagan Navigation ; are they defined by Act ?—They are.

840. Let us have them ?—In the Schedule to the Act of 1843.

841. One thousand eight hundred and seventy-three, is it not ?—The Act of 1873 refers to the Schedule of 1843, " For every boat, barge, or other vessel having no cargo on board and navigating the Lagan Navigation or any part thereof, either upwards or downwards, or in which any goods, merchandise or commodities, or any matter whatsoever not exceeding 15 tons, shall be carried, any sum not exceeding 1 *s.* 3 *d.* per mile. For every boat, barge, or other vessel navigating the Lagan Navigation, or any part thereof, either upwards or downwards, in which any goods, merchandise, or commodities, or any matter whatsoever exceeding 15 tons, shall be carried, any sum not exceeding the rate of 1 *d.* per ton per mile."

842. Now the rates on the Ulster Canal are much higher ?—Yes, the rates on the Ulster Canal are considerably higher.

843. I have a statement before me here of the rates : " To Benburb, a distance of 6 miles, 5 *d.* per ton ; Caldon, 14 miles, 6 *d.* per ton ; Middletown, 19 miles, 10 *d.* per ton ; Monaghan, 25 miles, 1 *s.* 6 *d.* per ton " ?—Yes, the Lagan rate, for 27 miles, at present is 9 *d.*

THE RIGHT HONOURABLE JAMES STANSFELD HERE TOOK THE CHAIR.

844. *Mr. Russell.*) The point pressing on me is this ; there is considerable complaint regarding the rates, not only the present rates, but the lighters returning are subject to very heavy haulage dues. Is that so on the Lagan Navigation ?—On the Lagan we charged nothing at all for empty boats returning.

845. The

845. The complaint of the people at Benburb and Caledon, and that way, is not only as regards excessive rates, but lockage dues in returning; there are four or five locks in the short distance to Benburb?—There are.

846. They have to pay 6 d. or 1 s. at each lock?—Yes.

847. What proposal have you to make with regard to that?—I think, as I understand it, the present Act enables us only to charge the same as we have been charging under the Lagan Act.

848. They have no dues returning for empties?—As a matter of practice we never charge anything at all. I have read the provision in the Act for charging. We do not make any charge for light boats.

849. You propose to make it exactly the same all through?—We have not been charging so, but the intention is to assimilate the tolls.

850. Col. Saunderson.] In this sub-section you cannot charge more on the Ulster part of the canal than you do on the Lagan Canal?—No.

851. You cannot exceed the rates authorised?—That is what we take it to be. Perhaps Mr. Williams can explain it better.

Chairman.] Are there any rates in this Bill not contained in the Lagan Navigation Act. Would it be a rate or a toll.

852. Mr. Russell.] Does they call them.—It would come under the head of tolls.

853. I am not satisfied with this 2nd sub-section at all?

854. Mr. Arthur O'Connor.] Have you no tolls on the Lagan. Have you no locks?—Twenty-seven locks. We do not charge for light boats or empty boats coming back through those locks.

855. Is that in accordance with some particular direction in the Act of 1843 or 1873?—No, I have just read the Clause. It says, "For every boat, barge, or other vessel having no cargo on board and navigating the Lagan Navigation or any part thereof, either upwards or downwards, or in which any goods, merchandises, or commodities, or any matter whatsoever not exceeding fifteen tons shall be carried, any sum not exceeding 1 s. 3 d. per mile." As a matter of practice we do not charge it.

856. There is nothing to prevent your charging at the rate of 1 s. 3 d. for the empties on the Ulster?—I take it this would give us authority to do so.

857. Mr. Russell.] I will read this paper before the Committee to show how those interested in it are affected. Mr. McKean, of Benburb, writes to me. "The present rates charged on coal and such like commodities is, as under, to Benburb, six miles, 8 d. per ton; Caledon, 14 miles, 6 d. per ton; Middletown, 19 miles, 10 d. per ton; Monaghan, 26 miles, 1 s. 3 d. per ton; upwards, 1 s. 8 d. per ton. The above include lockage; you will perceive, that the shorter the distance used the rates are higher in proportion; see why, I do not know; my opinion is it should be a mileage rate, say half-penny per mile; this would make it more equitable, and not place a premium on those only using the first five miles"?—That is the principle on which we have power to charge; we are hindered from charging more than a mileage rate.

858. "When lighters are returning empty a charge of 6 d. is put on for each lock; most of the locks are upon the first six miles; I think there are eight locks, which means 4 s. lockage for an empty lighter." That is very heavy for the man on the first six miles——

859. Colonel Saunderson.] Is that higher than the usual charge on the canal; do you know what it is on the other Irish canals?—I do not know.

860. Chairman.] I think I understood you to say that besides the remuneration for carriage and hauling, the rates for carriage and hauling are to be approved in writing by the Commissioners; whereas there is in the Lagan Navigation Act a rate you must not exceed that rate over the whole system?— I take that to be the meaning of it.

861. There would be other charges than those mentioned for hauling and for those rates mentioned in the Lagan Navigation Act?—I do not know.

862. Is there any lockage in the Lagan?—We do not make any charge apart

apart from the tolls: "The Company may take remuneration for such carriage
and haulage, so that the rates in respect of the carriage be approved in writing
by the Commissioners."

863. In the earlier part of the sub-section the rates in respect of carriage
must be approved by the Commissioners, but there are rates for hauling, and it
leaves out any tolls or rates not in respect of carriage or haulage and not
included in the Lagan Navigation Act. I think it wants more general
terms?— —

Mr. *Russell*.] I think so too.

864. *Chairman*.] You must either define and limit your power of levying the
tolls or rates, or we must refer it to some body who may approve?— We shall
be glad to receive any suggestion from the Committee.

865. Mr. *Arthur O'Connor*.] Do you know who laid down the existing rate on
the Ulster Canal?—The Commissioners.

866. Then the Commissioners would be likely to approve the existing rates?
—I am quite certain the Company would wish to reduce the rates, because they
are prohibitory, so far as I know.

867. Mr. *Russell*.] This gentleman says: "If five tons of cargo is put in,
say stone, sand, or any such, the tolls would only be 2 s. 6 d. I cannot see any
consistency in this; I think lockage should be abolished, and if returned empty,
should go free; say, pay 2 s. 6 d. to pass her through?"—I think there is
something of that sort.

868. *Chairman*.] Do you call that lockage?—We call it all toll; we do not
make any distinction.

869. Mr. *Arthur O'Connor*.] You have the right to take and receive tolls
and lockage and quayage and storage?—Yes.

870. Lockage is a term used in the Act?—Yes.

871. And duties arising under the provisions of the Act?—Yes.

872. *Chairman*.] How would this do: "The Company may take remuneration for such carriage and hauling, so that the rates of tolls or charges in respect
of carriage, haulage, lockage, or for any other purpose, shall not exceed such as
are authorised in the Lagan Navigation Act, 1873, and shall be approved in
writing by the Commissioners?—I do not think the Company would object to
that.

873. Mr. *Arthur O'Connor*.] Mr. Rea has already told us that the Company
propose to reduce the rates which they recognise as prohibitive?—There is
always a maximum rate, and the maximum allowed in the Lagan would not be
too high for the Ulster Canal.

874. Mr. *Russell*.] What do you think of a mileage rate of a halfpenny per
mile?—I do not think we should be bound to do that, because the rates, varying
according to the circumstances, it would alter all our arrangements in the
Lagan.

875. So that the rates, tolls, or charges in respect of carriage, haulage, lockage, or otherwise, shall not exceed such as are authorised in the Lagan Navigation Act, 1873, and shall be approved in writing by the Commissioners;
there is no lockage in the Lagan?—No; practically we call it all tolls.

876. Mr. *Arthur O'Connor*.] The rates on the Lagan Canal are already made
with the consent in writing of the Commissioners of Public Works?—Yes;
I think there is a feeling that the rates are lower in the Lagan.

877. Mr. *Russell*.] You told us that they are lower?—I think the public
would confirm it; we have no complaints about them.

The Committee proceeded to consider the clauses.

878. Mr. *Arthur O'Connor*.] I see that there is a note that the Company ask
for powers as common carriers for the public only, but they are intending to
act

act as traders through the Secretary opening depôts at various towns and villages for the sale of coal and other commodities, thus putting up an unfair competition with local merchants; I do not know if that is an adverse note or a friendly note; is it true?—At the present time I have been acting somewhat in that way, because the Company had no power to own lighters at all, and I have been acting as any other trader, paying my tolls along both canals, because they had no power to own boats.

879. Then the Company do propose to act as traders?—They have taken power, but they have had no consultations or discussions as to what they will do.

880. It is by the Company opening depôts?—There is no intention of the sort that I know of.

[The Committee further proceeded to consider clauses up to Clause 7.]

Mr. *Russell.*] This involves the leases and the notice to the public bodies.

Mr. *Arthur O'Connor.*] If the tenants of the Company wish to purchase their holding, you would have to get a separate Act of Parliament.

881. Mr. *Russell.*] As I understand it, the Company are willing, and the Company were prepared, either to allow the tenants to purchase or have the leases at the present rents?—We have a clause drawn to that effect.

882. You also offered, in your evidence on the last day, to insert that, in the event of the Company giving up the canal, notice should be given to the grand juries and public bodies of their intention?—We have embodied it in the clause.

883. Mr. *Arthur O'Connor.*] The Company would not object to a clause drafted for the purpose of protecting the tenants with respect to their improvements, and they would not object to the clause allowing the tenants to purchase?—We bind ourselves to that.

884. Mr. *Russell.*] They did that last time, and the leases were to be renewed at the present rents?—This is a rough copy of what we propose (*producing the same*).

885. Is this a new clause in place of Clause 7?——

Sir *Richard Wyatt.*] Yes.

Chairman.] "Subject to the proviso hereinafter-mentioned, the Company shall not sell, lease, or otherwise dispose of the said canals, or either of them, or of any land or property held on account thereof without the authority of Parliament, and without first giving notice in writing to the several secretaries for the time being of the Grand Juries of Armagh, Tyrone, Monaghan, and Fermanagh: Provided that nothing herein contained shall prevent the Company from leasing any lands or houses not required for the purpose of the Lagan Navigation, or for the purposes of the said canals or either of them, and the Company shall, subject to the approval of the Commissioners, signified in writing under the hand of their secretary, either continue all existing leases on the Tyrone Navigation at the rents existing at the time of the passing of this Act, or if the lessees require it, give them a right of purchase of their interests."

886. Mr. *Arthur O'Connor.*] You limit that to the Tyrone Navigation?—We do not know of any leases in the other. They are all in the five miles.

887. There may be tenants, although no leases. Are there any exceptions?—There is no provision for tenants who hold small holdings which may be required for navigation purposes.

888. They are the very men who most require protection; men who have made homes for themselves?—There is nothing of that sort. A thing of that sort is covered by a lease.

889. I thought you said there were exceptions; tenants who had not leases?
a. 2098.　　　　　　　　　　E 2　　　　　　　　　　　—Some

—Some one might have a small piece for grazing, which might be desirable for the Company to have. I do not know there are such cases, but we do know there is nothing in the shape of property or houses which is not covered by the lease.

Mr. *Russell.*] I have heard of nothing involving this question. They have power to grant these leases at the present rents, subject to the Board of Works.

890. *Chairman.*] Is there any objection to any lease, existing leases or tenancies?—There might be some things changing from year to year. They are trifling things; there are no houses or anything of that sort which it would be a hardship for any one to give up.

891. Mr. *Russell.*] This is the Ulster Canal?—We do not know of any tenancies.

892. Mr. *Arthur O'Connor.*] Therefore you might be trespassing on a right without knowing it?—We do not know there are leases of any consequence.

893. There might be some kind of occupying tenancy without a lease; the lease is the exception?—We do not know of anything except trifling things.

894. Mr. *Russell.*] " Provided that nothing herein contained shall prevent the Company from leasing or continuing any existing leases, and the Company shall, subject to the approval of the Commissioners signified in writing under the hand of the secretary." Those are the words you object to. I should prefer the clause this way: "The Company shall either continue all existing leases in the Tyrone navigation at the rents existing at the time of the passing of the Act, or if the lessees require it, give them a right to purchase their interest." Nothing was said on the last day about the Board of Works, and I do not know what the Board of Works may say. It seems to give the Board of Works a power which I do not see they should have?—As a matter of fact the Board of Works say they would recommend us to do it. There would be no objection to striking the words out.

895. Mr. *Arthur O'Connor.*] My point is that this protection is extended only to those who now hold leases; if there are others who do not hold leases they ought to be protected, and I cannot see why if the Company say there are no such persons there should not be words inserted, which cannot injure the Company, to protect any such cases that may exist?—I think there are some such things as rights of way which we should not be bound to give.

896. You could always say "saving rights of way"?—There is nothing more serious than something of that sort.

897. These people are not represented here; you are dealing with a large piece of property 44 miles long, and the chances are there must be some occupying tenants, and you may be depriving them of their rights——

Mr. *Macartney.*] What rights could they have which are not protected under the Land Act of 1881 ?

898. Mr. *Arthur O'Connor.*] They might not have leases but they might be as big holders as the leaseholders and yet not have leases?—I do not think there are any such cases at all.

899. You do not know there are not?—I could almost say there are not.

Mr. *Russell.*] It would be hardly fair to bind the company down neck and crop in every pettifogging case.

900. Mr. *Arthur O'Connor.*] The leaseholders are to be protected, and some are very small. It is not a pettifogging matter to the unfortunate men who hold the land?—The leaseholders have buildings on the ground; in these cases they are not of that kind.

Sir *Richard Wyatt.*] The great objection to creating a property, unless it comes within the general law (if you put something into a special Act of Parliament)

Parliament) is that it enables them to put the companies to enormous expense, shewing that they would have no portion of the costs of the arbitration to pay, where there is the express statutory power given to them. If they have any rights the general Act would be quite sufficient to protect them. I mean any remote interest.

Mr. Arthur O'Connor.] This is a Bill dealing with property. All you want it to execute that, while one property is being created, it shall not be unduly at the expense of other existing property. I do not see the objection; it cannot hurt the company.

Mr. Macartney.] The navigation is existing, and if they had any rights they had the rights as against the former owners of the navigation, and as against the Commissioners in whom the navigation is now vested, and those rights, such as they exist, cannot be destroyed by this Act. If they had any other rights, they are protected by the Land Law of Ireland.

901. *Mr. Arthur O'Connor.*] If that is true the leaseholders would not require special interest; they are able to protect their interest, and there may be other men living along that slip of 44 miles who equally want protection; we know of the existence of leaseholders, because they have made themselves heard, but the witness admits he is not prepared of his own knowledge to say that there are no people occupying without leases?—In either case they are only tenants from year to year, and the Board of Works could terminate the arrangement at any time.

902. Only tenants from year to year?—Year to year.

903. That is the position of all tenants in Ireland?

Mr. *Russell.*] The best way is to draft an amendment to that, and put it to the vote.

The Committee proceeded further to consider the clause.

Chairman.] "And the Company shall continue all existing leases on the Tyrone Navigation at the rents existing at the time of the passing of this Act, provided that the lessees shall be entitled at any time to purchase their interest." Is that form of words sufficiently definite to give a right of purchase; how do you give them a right of purchase without reference to terms?

Sir Richard Wyatt.] I think the enactment that they should have a right to purchase would give them power to enforce it by ordinary process of the Court.

Mr. *Arthur O'Connor.*] What would be the ordinary process of the Court?

Sir Richard Wyatt.] They would ask for specific performance, and if the Company declined to convey to them, the Court would compel them to do so.

Mr. *Arthur O'Connor.*] Would you, as a lawyer, say they would have a right to an action for specific performance under such circumstances?

Sir Richard Wyatt.] I think so.

Mr. *Arthur O'Connor.*] Do you know a case in which such action has been brought?

Sir Richard Wyatt.] I never saw such a clause.

Witness.] This is the clause they asked for.

903.* Mr. *Arthur O'Connor.*] I thought you brought it?—It is quite in accordance with what they have asked for.

Mr. *Russell.*] "The Company shall continue all existing leases on the Tyrone Navigation at the rents existing at the time of the passing of this Act,

Act, provided that the lessees shall be entitled at any time to purchase their interest." The option is clear; you are either bound to do one or the other.

Chairman.] The clause will give them a right; the Company will not give them the right.

Mr. Haley.] The Company either give them the lease or the right, one or the other alternative.

Chairman.] I daresay it would be capable of interpretation. I come to this: "The Company shall permit them."

Mr. Arthur O'Connor.] The Company shall have a right.

Sir Richard Wyatt.] Perhaps the better plan really would be to say "shall have the right to purchase their interest at such a price as shall, failing agreement, be settled by arbitration in the manner prescribed by the Lands Clauses Consolidation Act 1845."

Chairman.] I should be inclined to think it will do now.

Mr. Arthur O'Connor.] The Company shall continue all existing leases.

Chairman.] Continue all existing leases in the Tyrone Navigation.

Sir Richard Wyatt.] If you say "they shall," the antecedent being lessees, that will do. But suppose the lessees did not exercise the right of purchase exactly "at any time." First of all they are to be continued as lessees. "If at any time" they should desire to purchase they may do so.

Mr. Arthur O'Connor.] I have no objection to any verbal alterations. What you really want to do is to secure to the tenant the right of purchase at any time, and failing the exercise of that right, a second right to continue on the terms of his existing lease.

Sir Richard Wyatt.] I do not think it should be in the disjunctive. It should be "And if at any time."

Chairman.] This is what you mean: the Company shall continue all existing leases on the Tyrone Navigation at the rents existing at the time of the passing of this Act, providing that the lessees shall be entitled at any time to purchase their interest.

Sir Richard Wyatt.] It would read better "And if at any time the lessees." This is an empowering Clause, and it says the lease shall be continued and if at any time they desire to purchase the rights they shall be at liberty to do so.

The Committee proceeded further to consider the Clause.

904. Mr. Russell.] With regard to Clause 8, what was the term?—Thirty-one years.

905. It is a lease of 999 years, instead of 31?—Yes.

Mr. Arthur O'Connor.] Do you not think you could have inserted what you mentioned a little time ago about the minimum uniform depth of five feet.

Mr. Russell.] It would come in about line 8.

Mr. Arthur O'Connor.] In connection with the work of the repairs.

Chairman.] It is in continuance of the Lagan Navigation Acts.

Mr. Arthur O'Connor.] That would mean the work being done.

Sir

Sir *Richard Wyatt.*] This is merely continuing the provisions of the Act which at present have but 31 years, and it declares that those Acts so limiting the time shall be read as if 999 years had been inserted. That is only a continuance of the Act. I think it would come in better at the end.

Mr. *Arthur O'Connor.*] It is not merely a continuing clause; it is a clause continuing the Lagan Navigation Act, but upon conditions, which conditions are conditions precedent. If you make the deepening of the Canal throughout five feet as a condition precedent, you secure the deepening and you do not spoil the drafting of the clause.

Chairman.] All you accomplish is this, that if you do not deepen it five feet they do not get the prolongation of the Lagan Act.

Mr. *Arthur O'Connor.*] It would be a great object to continue it.

906. *Chairman.*] Now we are dealing simply with prolonging the Navigation Act. Your phraseology is, "The said Acts shall continue in force for the term of 999 years from the date of the said transfer taking effect, in like manner as if the term hereby limited for the continuance of the said Acts were substituted in the Lagan Navigation Act, 1843." Then how did the Lagan Act of 1878 deal with the original term in the Act of 1843?—It did not make any alteration in the term. It renewed the Act again for another term of 31 years.

Sir *Richard Wyatt.*] The Act of 1843 was for a limited term, and when that was about to expire they came to Parliament and obtained an extension of the term.

Mr. *Arthur O'Connor.*] Section 2 of the Lagan Navigation Act, 1878, says, "The Lagan Navigation Act 1843, as amended by this Act, and this Act, shall be read together as one Act, and shall be and continue in force for the term of 31 years from the passing of this Act, and until the end of the Session of Parliament next ensuing after the expiration of that term, and the Lagan Navigation Act 1843, shall be read and have effect as if throughout that Act the period by this Act limited for the continuance thereof were in that Act mentioned or referred to instead of the period of 31 years from the passing of that Act, and the Session of Parliament mentioned in Section 223 of that Act shall be deemed to mean the second Session of Parliament next ensuing after the expiration of 31 years from the passing of this Act."

Chairman.] My point is this: the proposal here is to extend the Lagan Navigation Act for the term of 999 years. Having done that, you go on to say that this extension shall take effect: "In like manner as if the term hereby limited for the continuance were substituted"; that is, if 999 years were inserted in the Act of 1843, and in the Act of 1878 you get rid of that term and substitute another.

Sir *Richard Wyatt.*] All the operative parts of the powers are in the Act of 1843. The Act of 1878 is merely a continuation of the terms with reference to what was authorised to be done under the Act of 1843.

Chairman.] Then you are satisfied?

Sir *Richard Wyatt.*] Perfectly satisfied.

The Committee proceeded further to consider the clause.

Mr. *Russell.*] What will happen if any of these contingencies happen after the expiration of the time fixed in the Act of 1878?

Mr. *Arthur O'Connor.*] Then their powers cease.

Sir Richard Wyatt.] Yes.

Chairman.] Then as to Section 9.

907. *Mr. Arthur O'Connor.*] Section 68, of the Act of 1843, says, that the "moiety of the excess of the company's income above 1,000 l. a-year, after payment of charges and interest on money borrowed, to be laid out and set apart for improvement of navigation, subject to inspection, &c. of Commissioners of Public Works." Section 4, of the Act of 1873, is an amendment of Section 68, "notwithstanding anything in the Act of 1843 contained, such sum as may be necessary of the said sum of 2,188 l. 0 s. 6d., or such other sum as at the date of the passing of this Act." That has reference to some transitory state of things. What is the amendment in 1873?—The Act of 1873, Clause 4.

908. *Sir Richard Wyatt.*] It has reference to the reserve fund?—Under that clause the Company had to set apart a moiety for the purpose of carrying out the works. There were certain millowners on the Lagan Canal who thought we might injure ourselves by the Ulster Canal, and instead of that they asked us to put aside a sum every year. That is the intention of the clause.

909. *Mr. Arthur O'Connor.*] How do these clauses in the Act of 1843 and the Act of 1873 now operate. The first provides "Moiety of the excess of the Company's income above 1,000 l. a year, after payment of charges and interest on money borrowed, to be laid out or set apart for improvement of navigation"?—Yes.

910. Do you do that still?—Yes, we have over 1,200 l. a year; a moiety over 1,200 l.

911. The Act of 1873 says: "Interest not exceeding four per cent. per annum on any moneys borrowed by the Company for the purposes of the said navigation shall exceed the sum of 1,200 l., the Company shall not be required to lay out and expend in new works, or to set aside for improvements, any part of such clear yearly income"?—That is increasing the amount. Under the old Act we were allowed to earn 1,000 l. and set apart half the balance; under the new Act we are allowed to earn 1,200 l. and set apart half the balance.

912. That is what you do now?—Yes.

913. Set apart 600 l. a year?—No. Say we earn 1,500 l., the difference between 1,200 l. and 1,500 l. is 300 l. We are required to set apart half that difference for new works. Under this present clause, no matter what we earn, we are bound to set apart a certain sum for new works every year. It is a clause against us, but we agreed to it.

Chairman.] Clause 9.

Mr. Arthur O'Connor.] The Board of Trade is not a desirable authority to bring in. We have not a Board of Trade in Ireland except for lighthouses.

Sir Richard Wyatt.] It is a mere ministerial act.

Mr. Arthur O'Connor.] The introduction of the Board of Trade would be out of the ordinary course.

914. *Mr. Macartney.*] An ordinary arbitrator under the Board of Works?—The arbitration is between the Board of Works and the Company.

Mr. Arthur O'Connor.] It must be somebody else. It ought not to be the Board of Trade.

Sir Richard Wyatt.] I may mention the Board of Trade is so constantly applied to to appoint an arbitrator, that they have a list of professional men, and they take them in the order in which they stand on the list.

Mr. Arthur O'Connor.] That is for England?

Sir Richard Wyatt.] Yes. It is a mere ministerial act. You might say,

say, "To be appointed by the President of the Institution of Civil Engineers."

Mr. *Arthur O'Connor.*] I object to the Board of Trade, not in England but in Ireland.

Mr. *Russell.*] Say the Lord Lieutenant.

Chairman.] Is that usual?

915. Sir *Richard Wyatt.*] Then this difficulty arises; who is to pay him? If he is appointed by the Lord Lieutenant, the Lord Lieutenant would have to pay him? There is a provision for payment under the clause, "Shall be paid out of the said funds."

916. As a matter of fact, it is not usual to impose a duty of that kind on the Lord Lieutenant without his sanction?—I think the Board of Trade was only put in because they could not think of any other body to put in.

Mr. *Russell.*] I see no reason why you should not put in the Lord Lieutenant, it is quite common to put it into Acts of Parliament.

Sir *Richard Wyatt.*] I do not remember any instance of that kind.

Chairman.] You have got the Treasury in already.

Mr. *Arthur O'Connor.*] I do not object to the Treasury.

Chairman.] "Shall be paid out of the said funds, or by the Company out of their other funds, or as the Commissioners acting as arbitrators may direct."

Mr. *Russell.*] What about deepening the canal five feet?

Chairman.] That will come in before Clause 11, after Clause 10.

The Committee proceeded further to consider the clauses.

917. *Chairman.*] The question raised in my mind the other day was whether this might happen that you might have some drainage scheme. The Bann Drainage, which should make their canal unnavigable, that a Company might have a claim against the Bann Navigation Scheme for the drainage to their canal, but they might pocket the proceeds of that claim, and might say, the canals are not navigable, and they are forfeited and revert to you the Commissioners, and so they get out of the bargain. Then I say, "The reverter of the said canal to the Commissioners shall not operate as a discharge to the Company from any debts, liabilities, or obligations of the Company; and that they should be liable for having made made default, and not be absolved by forfeiture of the canal?—With regard to the first proposition, in case there should be any physical impossibility in getting five feet of water, would that proposition bind us. The engineer who has given the estimate says it is possible to do it, but engineers are sometimes wrong.

918. Mr. *Russell.*] Would it be any use to you?—Not very much.

919. Colonel *Saunderson.*] Five feet is the minimum depth of water?—Yes.

Chairman.] We had a considerable discussion on what might be the effect of the Bann scheme of drainage, whether the company might get the damages and then throw up the canal.

Mr. *Macartney.*] It could only take place on the removal of one weir. As long as one weir is left the water cannot be affected, and the navigation is absolutely secure.

Chairman.] Whatever obligation the company has undertaken to the Commissioners they ought not to be absolved from, simply by throwing up the canal.

Sir Richard Wyatt.] Suppose it became physically impossible to keep it open by the act of some other body.

Mr. Arthur O'Connor.] That would be a sufficient plea; you would only have to prove *force majeure*.

Chairman.] All I say is that the reverter shall not operate as a discharge. They may be discharged by other facts, but not by the mere fact of throwing up the canal.

Sir Richard Wyatt.] The reverter is the protection to the Company. If they find they cannot do what is required of them to be done, then it is to revert back to the Commissioners. They will have lost all their money if during the next 10 years they find they cannot keep the navigation open, and in fact become bankrupt; then it is to revert back to the Commissioners; that is the bargain; it is like a right of re-entry in a lease. If a tenant does not do certain things the lessor is entitled to re-entry, and if we do not perform our duties it is to revert back to the Commissioners, and there is an end of the thing.

Mr. Arthur O'Connor.] This is put in Clause 3, Sub-section B, as a penalty to be enforced upon the non-performance of the covenant by the Company. Now you say this thing which is inserted as a penalty is a protection to the Company.

Colonel Saunderson.] I understand the clause to be this: If by some action of the Government or somebody else the level of the lock is lowered, and the navigation is destroyed, this Company, which would become derelict and bankrupt, would be at the pains and penalties of not carrying out a contract which they are prevented from doing by the action of somebody.

Mr. Arthur O'Connor.] They get compensation.

The Committee further considered the clause.

Sir Richard Wyatt.] I do not want the Act to be a dead letter; if you enact it, it shall be at times five feet, and it is not five feet at times, there will be a difficulty.

920. *Mr. Macartney.*] I do not think there will be any engineering difficulty in getting the water?—I think it is a question.

921. There is no difficulty about it?—We hope so, and expect so.

922. The Upper Bann would not be affected by any drainage?—No; but we do not get our supply there.

Chairman.] The precaution might be inserted in the agreement itself.

Sir Richard Wyatt.] You must positively it shall be five feet at all times.

Chairman.] There was to be a provision of that kind inserted. The company shall undertake to execute to the satisfaction of the Commissioners such works as repairs. They have to execute them to the satisfaction of the Commissioners.

Sir Richard Wyatt.] Yes.

Chairman.] What I say is, that shall include giving the Ulster Canal 5 feet way from end to end.

Sir Richard Wyatt.] That is a positive declaration in the Act that the agreement shall contain that.

Mr. Macartney.] The whole navigation depends on it.

923. *Mr. Russell.*] I shall not consent to anything short of five feet; the canal is useless without it?—It is the clear intention to give five feet.

Chairman.]

Chairman.] The question seems to me to be this: are we content that at any moment the company shall be able to throw the whole thing up, because, if they can throw it up, and be quit of their obligation, they may choose their own time for throwing it up. A considerable property is made over to them practically for the purpose of improving it, and maintaining the improvement in the public interest. Ought we not to take some guarantee that they shall fulfil that trust.

Colonel *Saunderson.*] If it only means that I do not object to it.

924. *Chairman.*] "The reverter of the said canal to the Company shall not operate as a discharge to the Company of any debts, liabilities, or obligations of the Company"?—I think if the failure of the canal comes through anything we could not control it would be rather hard on us to have this additional burden put upon us.

925. Mr. *Arthur O'Connor.*] Could you suggest anything in such a case?—I do not think it is at all likely if such a thing occurred by the lowering of the lock.

926. Have you got compensation?——

927. Mr. *Halsey.*] The reverter only refers to default being made by the Company in such undertaking. If you lost your water through Lough Neagh being drained, it would not be your fault?—If that is the understanding, I do not think there is any objection to it.

The Committee further considered the clauses up to Clause 12.

928. Mr. *Arthur O'Connor.*] On Clause 12 I wish to ask, have you the last balance-sheet of the Company by you?—Yes (*producing the same*).

929. The balance in hand was larger than it had been. "Balance carried to next account 1,430 *l.*?—Yes.

930. This does not show outstanding liabilities?—No.

931. So that it is not a statement of accounts at all?—Yes.

932. It is a statement of receipts and expenditure?—Yes.

933. But it does not show what your liabilities are?—Yes, they are all stated there. That is the income and expenditure. This is the balance-sheet.

934. How do you show your liabilities in this statement?—It is all there. The debtor column, "Ulster Bank" so much; "cash in hand" so much; and "materials."

935. You do not call cash in hand a liability?—The assets and liabilities are set out.

936. You have a balance in hand of 1,970 *l.*?—Yes.

937. What are your liabilities; what debts do you owe?—All in that column; those are our debts.

938. Loans from Commissioners?—Yes.

939. The Bank you owe 20 *l.*?—Yes.

940. Dean and Chapter of Down, 6 *l.*?—Yes.

941. Stock is not a debt; that is an asset?—Yes.

942. Have you real liabilities not shown there?—No.

943. Where are the expenses in connection with the promotion of this Bill?—They are there; Ulster Canal Account, 304 *l.*

944. There is an item 450 *l.*?—Yes.

945. What is the date of this?—31st March 1863.

946. What is your total liability now?—£. 85,423 we are liable for. That is share capital and all.

947. I do not mean that; I mean the ordinary liabilities; the current liabilities?—About 5,000 *l.* altogether.

948. How much is included in that for legal expenses and promotion money?—There is no promotion money.

949. Amounts due to your agent?—We have no legal expenses at all, except what is incurred in connexion with this present Bill.

259. Does that amount to 1,500 l.?—No, nothing of the kind.

951. It is 450 l.?—That is all.

952. That was up to 31st March?—Yes.

953. Have you not been incurring liability in connection with this Bill even up to to-day?—Yes; but of course that cannot be included in that statement. It is only a trifle more.

954. What do you estimate your total liability in respect of this Act?—We have not estimated it at all; it depends on the Parliamentary agent's costs.

955. You are the secretary of the Company?—Yes; but I cannot tell what their bill is.

956. The costs of this Bill are to be paid by the Company?—Yes.

957. Then would your balance disappear in the costs of this Bill?—I do not understand the question.

958. Your balance in hand will disappear; it will not be sufficient to meet your liabilities?—Yes, more than sufficient.

959. The money you borrow under this Act is to be appropriated for works for the improvement of the canal, buildings, and subscribing to the Company for tramway purposes?—Yes.

960. No portion of the money borrowed under this Bill is available for paying promotion expenses?—No;

961. I want you to show me how, without trenching on borrowed money, you with your present balance will be able to meet your liabilities connected with this Bill?—With the 1,200 l. carried forward, we do not anticipate the expenses connected with this Bill will be anything like that.

962. Is your agent for the Bill the same as was the agent for the Government?—Yes.

963. Mr. *Bailey*.] I suppose if your expenses did exceed that you would take them out of your current receipts, and it would so far diminish your dividend to your shareholders?—Yes.

964. Mr. *Arthur O'Connor*.] Supplying your receipts with borrowed money?—No.

   The Committee proceeded to consider the remaining Clauses of the Bill.

   The Chairman was ordered to report on the Bill, with Amendments, to the House.

APPENDIX.